THE MAN OF BRONZE

Doc Savage's lifework was unusual—he had devoted himself to righting wrongs and thwarting evildoers in all parts of the world. He did not hire out his services. He never took a case unless a wrong was being done, and unless it appeared that the regularly constituted law authority was unable to cope with the malefactor. Within a very few years, Doc Savage and his group of five scientific assistants had built up a worldwide reputation. Doc Savage had also become something of a mystery name. He was sometimes called The Man of Bronze. The world knew he was a combination of scientific genius, muscular marvel and mental wizard. But not much else was known.

Bantam Books by Kenneth Robeson
Ask your bookseller for the books you have missed

About Doc Savage

DOC SAVAGE: HIS APOCALYPTIC LIFE
by Philip José Farmer

THE RED TERRORS

A DOC SAVAGE ADVENTURE

BY KENNETH ROBESON

BANTAM BOOKS · LONDON · TORONTO · NEW YORK

THE RED TERRORS

*A Bantam Book / published by arrangement with
Condé Nast Publications Inc.*

PRINTING HISTORY

*Originally published September 1938
in DOC SAVAGE MAGAZINE*

Bantam edition / July 1976

ISBN 0-553-06486-X

Published simultaneously in the United States and Canada

PRINTED IN THE UNITED STATES OF AMERICA

CONTENTS

Chapter I

THE RED MEN!

A sailor named Steve ate an apple, and killed thirty-eight men. By eating the apple, he killed the thirty-eight men just as effectively as though he had taken hold of the trigger of a machine gun and pumped lead into the victims. Steve's process, however, was a little slower and more terrible.

Steve bought his apple off a cart in Majunga, Madagascar. Apple vendors in Majunga have a habit of breathing on their apples when polishing them.

The merchant who breathed on Steve's apple had diphtheria.

Steve was a sailor on the steamer *Muddy Mary*. *Muddy Mary* was fairly fittingly named. Some of her crew said she should have been named Creaking Mary, or other things not so complimentary.

The *Muddy Mary* was an old hag of the sea, and like the old hags of the streets, she wandered around oceans, picking up a nickel here, a penny there.

She picked up Harry Day in Cape Town, South Africa. Harry Day was a man who had peculiarities of physical appearance which made him an easy person to remember; in other words, he was striking.

He had a great quantity of white hair, and each hair was as white as snow and as thick as a banjo string, and usually about six inches long. Every hair on his head also stood on end. His long face was a weather-beaten brown.

The effect was rather like an Indian with a headdress of white feathers. Also, Harry Day was sufficiently tall that he always cocked an eye at a doorway before he went through it, to see if it was high enough.

Harry Day was known all over the world as the deep-sea diver who went down to the U-71 when she lay trapped so deep that no other diver could make it.

Harry Day loaded his deep-sea equipment in the *Muddy Mary* hold, and the ship hoisted anchor, put out to sea and set a compass course for New Orleans.

The nicest thing that could be said about the *Muddy Mary's* speed was that she was slower than the itch. Even less could be said for her abilities in a storm, but she had one quality in common with the Rock of Gibraltar—every wave that came along hit her with everything it had, and she could take it.

The six lifeboats she carried could not take it. The storm that hit the *Muddy Mary* in the middle of the South Atlantic smashed every last lifeboat aboard, tore the life raft off the deckhouse and carried away most of the ring life buoys.

But by that time, the crew didn't care much. There were thirty-eight men, crew and officers, and Harry Day, the only passenger. Three fourths of them were in their bunks with diphtheria. Some of the men in the bunks were dead; the corpses were left lying because no one had time or energy to give them sea burial, what with each man on his feet having to do the work of three on their backs.

Life on the *Muddy Mary* became a hysteria of fear and fatigue. The unsick were so driven that they could not tell whether they had contracted diphtheria or not. They had dizzy spells brought on by utter tiredness, and were stricken with needless terror lest they had diphtheria.

"Poke" Ames, one of the engine-room black gang, was such a case. At five o'clock, he grew dizzy and nearly fell over. Thereafter he worked silently, mouthed prayers for salvation, and didn't pay attention to his duties.

It was seven o'clock approximately when Poke Ames accidentally closed the wrong valves from the boilers to blow a thirty-foot hole in the belly of the *Muddy Mary*.

A lot of sea water ran come through a thirty-foot hole.

Harry Day was in the forehold when the blast came, trying to spike down his heavy cases of diving equipment so that they would not be smashed by being tossed from one side of the ship to the other. He had just succeeded in securing every box so that it would not be broken when the explosion came and blew the cases loose again.

For thirty seconds—and seconds could be long after an explosion like that—Harry Day lay on his back and screamed. He didn't believe, like the American Indians, that you were a coward and a weak sister if you screamed when in pain.

Harry Day was in pain. His left arm had been broken in three places.

When he picked himself up to stagger, still screaming, to the bulkhead door which offered the only exit except a hatch that he couldn't reach, he got the screams scared out of him, for the blast had jammed the bulkhead door. He couldn't get it open! He was trapped! He could tell from the way the floor began slanting that the *Muddy Mary* would be on top of the Atlantic four or five minutes more at a generous most.

Harry Day didn't want to die. Several newspapermen and an article writer for a magazine had written that the deep-sea diver Harry Day was a man unafraid of death. They were wrong. When he was diving, Harry Day knew what he had to do to be safe, and knew that if he did it, he would be safe.

Right now, he knew he was going to die. He knew nothing could save him. He was trapped in a fast-sinking ship, in a sea so rough that he would not have been any better off on deck. He was going to die.

He wanted to live. The superficial was stripped from everything, and one raw reality was left: death! And Harry Day wanted to live more than he had ever wanted anything, and more than he could ever want anything again. He wanted to live! Even for a minute! A few seconds!

That was why Harry Day, in wild haste, put on the

diving suit he used for his deepest work. The suit was alloy steel re-enforced to withstand pressure. It was entirely self-contained; a mechanical "lung" supplied oxygen and purified exhaled air so it could be used again.

Harry Day, wearing the suit, resembled the cartoon pictures labeled "robot". Fortunately the suit was designed so it could be donned without external aid.

There was a telephonic device inside the helmet, and this ran to the amplifier. Earlier in the voyage, Harry Day had been demonstrating the communications arrangement to one of the *Muddy Mary*'s officers, and the amplifier and loud-speaker were still attached to the microphone inside the helmet.

In his nervous haste to turn on the "lung", he also turned on the communicator. The result was that every sound Harry Day made inside the all-metal diving suit as the ship sank was amplified and poured from the loud-speaker.

For a time, there was only the doomed man's breathing. He was doomed; he knew that. This was an unfrequented part of the Atlantic between South America and Africa, where soundings showed depths of thousands of feet. And Harry Day's diving suit, modern as it was, would not let him descend to a depth of even a thousand feet and live.

Harry Day's breathing was staccato. He panted. He also made a small sound occasionally, the kind of noise that men make when very terrified. Such a sound as soldiers make when watching a bomb fall toward them, or some dogs when they see a man with a club.

The old *Muddy Mary* was breaking slowly amidships and folding up. The floor slant grew steeper and Harry Day went sliding to one end of the hold. Boxes of equipment slid down and piled up on him. The hatch caved under water pressure. Tons of sea poured in. It was the pouncing roar of a deluge that chased things around in the hold and jostled the diver in his suit.

The old steamer broke completely apart in the middle with loud whistles of escaping air and rotten-egg reports of hatches caving. The two halves then sank. Madly driven waves, fighting bubbles, and flotsam were soon all that showed where she had been.

Harry Day lay in his alloy steel diving suit and waited for the end. He was wishing he hadn't seized these few seconds of life. They were the worst moments he had ever lived.

There was little movement as the ship sank. But the needle on the water-pressure gauge inside the diving suit hood kept creeping up. Harry Day watched the needle with eyes that seemed to be trying to get out of their sockets.

Unexpectedly, Day's half of the steamer rolled over again. There was a great shock as heavy equipment cases toppled across the hold and landed on the diver.

A compressor-case came down on Day's broken left arm. The case weighed three tons. It bent the metal diving-suit terribly, and more bones broke in the diver's arm with sounds like traps catching rats.

Harry Day fainted.

It was agony that brought Harry Day back to consciousness. Grinding, jerking, electric pain. Because he was so stupefied that he only knew he was being hurt, he yelled out in anger; but the anger turned to fear as he remembered he was in a ship that was sinking.

He had been senseless, but it must have been for only a few minutes, because it would not take long for the steamer to sink deep enough for pressure to crush his diving suit. Then he saw the luminous-dialed watch which was part of the instruments inside the hood.

The watch said it was nearly four hours since the ship sank.

Four hours! That couldn't be. Impossible! The water was thousands of feet deep all over this part of the Atlantic, according to the charts.

Harry Day peered at the luminous watch. Four hours was what it read. And there was nothing wrong with the watch. He had been careful to keep it wound and running as he visited the hold daily to see that his instruments were not being corroded by the salt air.

But four hours. It couldn't be!

Then he realized something had hold of one of his legs and was twisting, pulling.

Harry Day remembered two things, and neither one was pleasant. He remembered the giant octopuses which live at great sea depths. And he thought of a thirty-five foot shark he'd once seen.

Then he saw what had hold of him. What he saw was the last thing on earth he expected to see. It was not a shark or an octopus. The thing peered through the bullet-proof glass of the diving helmet at Harry Day's face.

"Oh, Mother of Mercy!" screamed Harry Day, and fainted.

Chapter II

DOCTOR COLLENDAR

Doctor Hugo Collendar was a man who had made mistakes. His first error was conceivably in being born at all, and that one was the most unfortunate, as far as the world was concerned. Everything that came afterward merely compounded and aggravated the situation.

Doctor Collendar had traits supposed to be desirable. He was persistent. He made up his mind at a very early age to be a doctor and surgeon, and he stuck to that and became one.

He was no coward, and that is also supposed to be a virtue. He did not let any such thing as fear of going to the penitentiary stand in his way when getting something he wanted. He was ambitious. He made up his mind to have a million dollars when he was forty. So have a lot of men. But Doctor Collendar was making good.

When the diver Harry Day disappeared, Doctor Collendar was not quite forty, and he wasn't far from having a million, either.

However, by that time Doctor Collendar had raised his sights. His goal was now unlimited millions—and power.

7

Bossing chauffeurs and butlers had given him a taste of telling men what to do, and he wanted to tell the world what to do, and have his word law.

Altering "Snig" Bogaccio's face was still another mistake. Doctor Collendar's desire to earn one hundred thousand easy dollars was the cause of that error.

He contracted to change Mr. Snig Bogaccio's face, fingerprints, and physical contour with plastic surgery so that the increasingly efficient Department of Justice could not find Bogaccio nor identify him if they did find him.

The operation was a great success. So much of a success that Snig Bogaccio sent one of his cronies around for the same treatment. Unluckily, the crony died. Snig Bogaccio was not aggravated; he understood it was just one of those things. He and Doctor Collendar remained good friends.

But the police found the body of Snig Bogaccio's crony and began investigating. Doctor Collendar had made some further mistakes in covering up, the first thing he knew, he realized he'd better be taking a vacation in some faraway place like Madagascar.

Doctor Collendar sailed on the *Southern Wind,* a craft advertised as a liner, but nearer a freighter with passenger accommodations. Destination Cape Town.

Nothing happened until the *Southern Wind* was approximately halfway across the South Atlantic.

Doctor Collendar was a tall collar ad. He was aware that he was handsome, and enhanced it by the way he dressed. His large blue eyes were afflicted with astigmatism, but he refused to wear glasses because he thought he didn't look well in them.

Since he couldn't see distinctly, he'd formed a habit of opening his eyes very wide at intervals. At such times, it was as though he had peeled two hard-boiled eggs.

The thing Doctor Collendar resented most about his enforced ocean voyage was the lack of suitable feminine companionship. There were nothing but homely females aboard.

He was standing at the rail, brooding about this lack, when there was a shout on the bridge.

"Distress signal!" yelled the voice on the bridge. "Distress signal! Hard off port bow!"

Doctor Collendar peeled eyes several times before he saw a spot of purplish light on the sea ahead. This flashed on and off methodically. The light would make three short flashes, three long flashes, then three more short ones. Doctor Collendar recalled that this was the international distress signal, S O S.

Southern Wind engines reversed the ship to a standstill. Searchlight beams lunged out from the bridge and licked the sea like anteaters' tongues. The lights did not disclose anything. A sea of some size was running, and it was obvious the sensible thing was to lower small boats and search. This was done.

Leaning against the rail, Doctor Collendar gave himself over to contemplation of the aspects of life, the lack of femininity aboard, and other more personal things. The fact that someone might be in distress on the dark windswept sea did not move him, except impersonally. He was cold to other people's misfortunes.

"Is there a doctor aboard?"

This inquiry came from behind Doctor Collendar. He turned at once to see who had spoken.

"We need a doctor badly," the voice added from the shadow of an awning. Doctor Collendar could not make out the person who spoke, peel his eyes as he would.

Doctor Collendar decided to deny that he was a doctor. Second thought reminded him he was chafing at the monotony of the trip, and it might be a diversion to keep his hand in practice.

"I am a doctor," he admitted.

"Surgeon or physician?" asked the voice.

"Both."

"Are you a pathologist?"

"Why, yes."

"Have you had much experience?" asked the voice.

"A great deal," said Doctor Collendar rather proudly.

"Then we are very fortunate to find you," the voice said.

The speaker stepped out of the shadows. Doctor Collendar stared. He could tell no more about the person than before! The unknown walked directly toward Doctor Collendar and held out a hand.

Too late, Doctor Collendar learned the other did not want to shake hands.

The tall form, draped from head to foot in something wet and clinging which had a dull purplish tint, took hold of Doctor Collendar's hand, and its clutch felt like a *thing*. The next instant, Doctor Collendar was seized in a grip of great strength.

Doctor Collendar yelled in fright.

"Help!" he bawled. "I'm being thrown overboard!"

His scream was heard on the bridge, and an officer cocked a searchlight on the spot.

Just as the light splattered across the scene, the two struggling figures went over the rail.

No one but Doctor Collendar saw the exact nature of the thing he was fighting.

The crew never forgot what Doctor Collendar screamed as he fell into the sea with his assailant. His words were:

"The thing is red!"

The steamer searched the vicinity for hours, without finding a trace of Doctor Collendar or his assailant.

Chapter III

THE BRONZE MAN

Clark "Doc" Savage, Jr., had heard of Doctor Collendar.

However, Doc Savage did not pay particular attention to the newspaper clipping concerning Doctor Collendar's peculiar death. That is, he did not give it *personal* attention. He came upon the clipping among many others which one or another of his five assistants had thought deserving of his attention and had placed on his desk.

Doc Savage passed the clipping to "Renny". Renny was Colonel John Renwick, a man with a pair of incredibly big fists, a voice equally as big, an unfailingly sad expression, and a reputation as one of the world's greatest engineers. Renny was one of Doc's five aids.

"Might have our Cape Town operative to question those on the *Southern Wind* concerning the disappearance of this Doctor Collendar," Doc Savage said.

Renny scrutinized the clipping.

"That shout about a red thing is kinda interesting," he said, sounding like a big bear in a small cave.

Renny then cabled the Cape Town operative, but

nothing substantial came of that. Not that the Cape Town operative wasn't efficient. He was. All Doc Savage's operatives, scattered in the far corners of the earth, were efficient.

All these highly efficient operatives of Doc Savage had one very peculiar thing in common: Each one could remember back just so far in his life, and no farther. There was not one of them who could recall any incident in his youth. More peculiar, none of these operatives could remember a period when he or she had been a desperate criminal.

The operatives were "graduates" of Doc Savage's unique "College" for curing criminals—an institution where the patient first underwent a remarkable brain operation which wiped out all memory of the past.

After the operation, the former criminals were educated to hate crime and to like being upright citizens. Many of the "graduates" became operative in the information-gathering agency which Doc Savage had created to aid him in his life's work.

Doc Savage's life's work was unusual.

His work was righting wrongs and thwarting evildoers in all parts of the world. He did not hire out his services. He never took a case unless a wrong was being done, and unless it appeared that the regularly constituted law authority was unable to cope with the malefactor.

Within a very few years, Doc Savage and his group of five scientific assistants had built up a world-wide reputation. Doc Savage had also become something of a mystery name. He was sometimes called "The Man of Bronze". The world knew he was a combination of scientific genius, muscular marvel and mental wizard. But not much else was known.

Newspaper reports concerning Doc Savage were usually so fantastically garbled that even the public didn't believe them.

The newspapers found it practically impossible to get any interviews with Doc Savage. The bronze man avoided publicity. The newspapers resented this.

At the time Doctor Collendar disappeared, the newspapers were resenting it more than usual.

A platoon of reporters and cameramen cornered "Long

Tom" and "Johnny", two of Doc Savage's group of five colleagues, in the lobby of a skyscraper, on the eighty-sixth floor of which the bronze man had his huge laboratory-library headquarters.

"We want a statement from Doc," said one of the reporters, "about the cure for cancer which he just invented."

"Doc hasn't invented any cure for cancer," Long Tom said.

Long Tom was Major Thomas J. Roberts, and he wasn't long. His height was average, and his general physical condition appeared to be much below average. He looked, in fact, like a hospital case of anemia.

This was deceptive, because Long Tom had never been ill, and he could whip ninety per cent of the men he met on the street. He was an electrical expert.

"Don't kid me!" said the reporter loudly. "Doc Savage just treated twenty-four cases of cancer and cured them!"

"Yes," Long Tom said, "but he treated a twenty-fifth case and didn't cure it."

"It looks like a pretty dang good average to me," stated the newspaperman.

"Doc gave you fellows one statement," Long Tom said, "in which he said he didn't want newspapers to arouse a lot of false hopes among cancer sufferers. Doc said the twenty-four cures he effected could be duplicated by any specialist." Long Tom frowned. "We're getting tired of these wild newspaper stories you print about Doc. This cancer business is typical. You came right out and said he had discovered a cure."

"Mistakes wouldn't happen," snapped the newshawk, "if Doc Savage would take us into his confidence."

"And let you publish stories about what he does?"

"Exactly."

"If he did that," Long Tom said, "he wouldn't live six months."

"Why not?"

"Because his enemies would learn all about his methods from reading your newspaper stories, and they'd get him sure."

"Doc has a lot of enemies, eh?"

"Everybody who is doing something wrong," said Long Tom, "is a potential enemy of Doc Savage."

"Who is Doc Savage's most outstanding enemy at present?" asked a newspaperman, fishing for a story.

Long Tom considered.

"I believe his prominent foe at the moment is a Mr. Lucifer," he said.

"Where does Mr. Lucifer live?"

"I believe in a place known as Tartarus."

The newshawk grew excited. "Look, what'd this Mr. Lucifer do that was wrong? What—"

"He's kiddin' you, Hank," interrupted another reporter.

"Eh?"

"Lucifer is the devil," said the reporter, "and Tartarus is another name for hell."

The first reporter glared indignantly.

"I resent such treatment!" he shouted. "We want an interview!"

At this point, Johnny spoke,

"An amphigourish pedantical pedagoguery," Johnny said calmly.

Johnny was William Harper Littlejohn, who was often described as being two men high and less than half a man wide. He carried a monocle magnifier which he never put in his eye, and he was an eminent archeologist and geologist, and an eminent user of big words.

The newspapermen looked at Johnny.

"*What?*" one of them gasped.

Long Tom said, "He means that you might as well save your breath."

With which Long Tom and Johnny took a dignified departure. Long Tom remarking audibly, "Hurry up! We promised to talk to Doc in a few minutes. He's waiting."

The newspapermen heard this remark. As a squadron, they fell in and trailed Long Tom and Johnny.

"They're doin' what we hoped they'd do," Long Tom chuckled.

Long Tom and Johnny entered what looked like a very dilapidated old car parked at the curbing. The machine was a sedan with a body vintage at least ten years outdated, and a general air which indicated its top speed might be at the most thirty-five miles an hour. Paint was peeling off its flanks.

"Some chariot," Long Tom muttered.

"A proficuous conveyance," Johnny said with dignity.

The very tall Johnny drove. Unhealthy-looking Long Tom drew a small case from his pocket, held it close to his cheek and spoke to it in a pleased tone.

"The reporters are all followin' us, Doc," he said. "The coast is clear for you to get away for that vacation."

"Very well, Long Tom," said a voice from the case, which contained a diminutive ultra-short-wave radio transceiver.

Doc Savage's voice was remarkable, even when reproduced by the tiny loud-speaker in the transceiver.

"Anything else for us to do?" Long Tom asked.

"No," Doc Savage said. "Unless something should develop, I will be back in a few weeks. In the meantime, you can reach me at Salisbury, on the eastern shore of Chesapeake Bay."

"O.K.," Long Tom said. "Good luck, Doc, on the vacation."

Long Tom replaced the transceiver in his pocket. He grinned at Johnny.

"That means Doc isn't goin' to his Fortress of Solitude," the electrical wizard remarked. "I'm glad of that. I'm always kinda worried when Doc goes to the Fortress."

For a change, Johnny spoke and used small words.

"Yes," he said, "something may happen to Doc up there sometimes, and that would be bad, because none of us have the slightest idea where this Fortress of Solitude is located, except that it is in the Arctic somewhere."

Long Tom turned around and examined several taxicabs holding pursuing newspapermen.

"Scribes," he said, "here's your surprise."

They fed the dilapidated old car gas, and the old heap came to life and went eighty miles an hour up a boulevard, making hardly a sound. It turned into a side street, took corners, and left the newspapermen feeling foolishly lost.

The scribes went back to Doc Savage's skyscraper headquarters.

"Doc Savage," they were informed, "has left the city."

When an elderly looking gentleman—he had flowing

white hair and a neatly clipped white Vandyke beard—
arrived in Salisbury, Maryland, center of the oyster
industry, no one gave him more than average attention.

The elderly gentleman had only one outstanding char-
acteristic that the public associated with Doc Savage;
He was a giant. He habitually walked with a stoop, but
even this did not disguise the fact that he had a figure
of Herculean proportions.

The newspaper-reading public knew that Doc Savage
was a giant man of bronze with straight bronze hair only
slightly darker than his skin, and eyes like pools of flake
gold that were vitally alive.

The white-haired, white-bearded gentleman who busied
himself studying oysters was not recognized as Doc Savage
for several weeks.

Doc had intended to return to New York after a
brief vacation—if studying oysters could be considered a
vacation. However, it was quiet around Salisbury, and
a relief not to be plagued by newspapermen and curious
people, and Doc remained overtime.

Another reason for staying was the importance of his
work in Salisbury. The oyster industry was being menaced
by a plague of starfish. The starfish fed on the oysters,
using a form of attack on the bivalve that was deadly.

The starfish approached an oyster, which, of course,
clamped its shell tight. The starfish would then crawl
upon the oyster, fix its sucking feet to the oyster's shell,
and begin exerting a pressure which was not great, but
which was inexorable.

Eventually the compression overcame the tired muscles holding the oyster's shell closed, after which the
starfish calmly turned its stomach inside out, wrapped it
around the unfortunate oyster, and began digesting.

Doc Savage hoped to develop a parasite which was a
natural enemy to the starfish and thus fight the scourge
of echinoderms.

He worked in Salisbury a few weeks; then his identity
was discovered, and a swarm of newspapermen arrived.
However, there was nothing of much reading value in a
scientific attempt to rid oysters of a natural enemy, and the
journalists departed.

It was nine weeks to the day after Doc Savage arrived

in Salisbury when a buzzing came from a case which stood in the little shack that the remarkable bronze man was using for his headquarters.

The buzzing meant that one of his men was seeking to get in touch with him by radio.

"Yes?" Doc Savage said into the microphone.

"This is Monk in New York," a squeaky voice said.

The voice was almost childish, but "Monk" was no child. Monk was a man practically as broad as tall, furred over with red hairs that resembled rusty shingle nails, and who could take a half dollar in his right hand and bend its two edges together, then duplicate the feat with his left hand. He was a skilled chemist, was this Lieutenant Colonel Andrew Blodgett "Monk" Mayfair.

"Doc," Monk said, "you remember that Doctor Collendar who disappeared in the middle of the South Atlantic, hollering something about, 'The thing is red!'?"

"Yes."

"Well, there was a fight on a waterfront street here last night that kinda reminded me of this Doctor Collendar."

"Reminded you? Why?"

"A taxi driver who saw the fight," Monk said, "claimed that there was one white man in the scrap and the fellow was fighting what the taxi man called 'something red.' I saw an item in the newspapers this mornin' and the stuff about somethin' red made me remember Doctor Collendar, so just for fun I went out to see the taxi driver.

"He said it was too dark to tell anything, except that something red was fightin' a white man. Then the white man got loose, and he fled past the taxi driver, and the driver got a good look at him."

Monk paused a few seconds for dramatic effect.

"Just for fun," he said, "I showed this hackman a picture of Doctor Collendar. And what do you think, Doc?"

Monk paused again for drama.

"Never mind the trimmings," Doc suggested.

"Well, the white man was Doctor Collendar," Monk said, "or so the hackman insisted."

"But Doctor Collendar disappeared off a ship in the South Atlantic two months ago," Doc Savage said.

"That's why I called you," Monk said. "It's queer, and I figured you'd be interested."

"The taxi driver might have made an error."

"I don't think so, Doc. He said this fellow he saw had a way of poppin' his eyes. The picture of Doctor Collendar that I showed the taxi driver didn't indicate any such thing. But I made inquiries. And that eye-poppin' was a habit of this Doctor Collendar."

Doc Savage did not say anything for a moment. During the interval, a weird and tiny sound came into existence. It rose and fell, at times hardly audible, at other times having considerable volume, and always with a quality of vague unreality that made it almost indefinable. It was as ethereal as the sounds of an arctic breeze among ice pinnacles.

"I shall be in New York in two hours," Doc Savage said abruptly.

Chapter IV

MENACE IN CRIMSON

It was a small newspaper item about the fight between a white man and some mysterious opponents who were unidentified except for reddish coloration. It was only two paragraphs.

Doc Savage read it, then asked, "Where did the fight occur?"

"On Yardarm Street near the East River," Monk said.

"That is near the Colonial-African Steamship Line piers," the bronze man remarked. "The firm operates the *Southern Wind* and other steamships."

Doc Savage handed the clipping to Monk. They stood in the bronze man's water-front boathouse-hangar which appeared outwardly an abandoned warehouse.

Doc had just taxied his small plane into the hangar and closed the doors with an electrical mechanism. The bronze man walked over to an instrument board, and threw a switch and said, "Ham!"

"Righto!" came from a loud-speaker on the board.

"Join us at the black sedan," Doc Savage said.

The loud-speaker said, "Righto!" again.

Doc Savage and the apish Monk strode to an object

19

which appeared to be a steel cylinder standing on end. They opened a door, and entered a padded chamber.

The bronze man closed the doors and operated a switch; there was a loud whistling, violent acceleration, a whining, then deceleration, and the bullet-like car came to a stop—it had passed through a pneumatic tube, under streets and buildings, for nearly a score of blocks.

Doc and Monk stepped out in the bronze man's garage, which was located in the basement of his skyscraper headquarters. "Ham" joined them, with Habeas Corpus and Chemistry.

Ham was Brigadier General Theodore Marley Brooks, who was always correctly dressed, who always carried an innocent-looking black cane with a sword inside, and who got outrageous fees when he practiced his profession of lawyer.

Ham's real career was that of a Doc Savage assistant. His hobby was quarreling with Monk. Ham shaded his eyes with a hand and peered dramatically at Monk.

"Great Jehoshaphat!" he exclaimed. "A perfect specimen of prehistoric man! Where'd you get it, Doc? Out of a tree?"

"You shyster!" Monk said. "I'll hit you over the head so hard you won't be able to tell the tacks in your shoes from the fillings in your teeth!"

The two glared at each other.

Following their example, Habeas Corpus and Chemistry sat down and also glared at each other. Habeas Corpus was a pig with long legs, extensive ears and an inquisitive snout. He was Monk's pet. Chemistry was Ham's pet.

According to Ham, Chemistry was a blue-blooded ape of direct descent from the house pets of ancient Mayan royalty. Monk's opinion of Chemistry's ancestry was different, and varied from day to day.

Doc Savage, with Monk and Ham and the two animals, entered a black sedan. Doc drove. The sedan did not look like the mobile fortress of armor plate and bulletproof glass that it was. They soon arrived at the Colonial-African steamship pier.

"Why, yes," admitted the chief officer of the steamer lying at the pier. "We got in from Cape Town, Africa, yesterday afternoon late."

Doc Savage asked, "Did you have any passengers who were unusual?"

"I'll say we did. We had—" The officer frowned. "Sorry. Against the rules to give out information to strangers."

Doc Savage made his identity known.

"You're Doc Savage!" the officer said. "That makes a difference."

"What about the unusual passengers?" Doc asked.

"Well, here's what happened," the chief officer said. "In Cape Town, a man rented an entire suite of cabins. Six cabins, to be exact. He had the windows covered, the doors barred, and nobody got a look inside the cabins all the way across the ocean."

"What kind of a looking man rented the cabins?"

The officer described Doctor Collendar.

"He's gone now, though," the officer added. "Disappeared after dark last night. I don't know what the immigration officials will do about it."

"Did you notice anything strange at any time?" Doc asked.

The officer considered.

"Well, there was one of the stewards who was babbling about something he saw at one of the cabin portholes," he said.

They called the steward for questioning.

"Hi dunno wot it was, gov'nor," the steward shuddered. "It was just a kind of 'orrible red smear of a thing!"

Doc Savage did not offer any words as he and his aids rode uptown in the black sedan. His two companions were disappointed, but not surprised. Doc Savage had a habit of keeping his own counsel. To kill time, Monk and Ham hashed things over in their bellicose fashion.

"Look, hairy ignorance," Ham said, "it would appear that this Doctor Collendar came back to the United States and brought something strange with him."

"You seem to be correct, you overdressed discredit to the law profession," Monk admitted.

"Of course, I'm right."

"Except that Doctor Collendar was dragged off a ship in mid-Atlantic and drowned," Monk pointed out.

"Depend on you to bring up a detail like that," Ham grumbled.

Doc's sedan came to a stop before a tall office building in the Wall Street area. Several times, Doc had consulted an envelope containing reports which his operatives had previously gathered as a matter of routine on Doctor Collendar.

"Doctor Collendar has offices in this building," the bronze man explained. "His rent was paid, and I understand they are still open."

The lobby director said Doctor Collendar's suite was 2117. The elevator operator recognized Doc Savage and ran past the floor in his excitement. The door of 2117 was unlocked.

"Blazes!" Monk ejaculated.

The interior of Doctor Collendar's office suite looked as though it had been the scene of one of the free-for-all fights which always came at the climax of movies fifteen years ago.

Chairs were smashed, tables upset, the desk upended, a spittoon bent, and the typewriter was on the floor in a nest of its own parts.

"This makes two fights," Monk remarked. "One was in the street near the steamship pier last night."

Doc Savage went over and examined the dampness of ink stains where a bottle had upset on the rug,

"This one happened about three hours ago," the bronze man judged from the wetness of the stains.

He picked up the typewriter. After he had studied it a moment, the strange, trilling sound came into being and ran up and down the musical scale. It followed no definite tune, and it had ventriloquial quality which made its exact source difficult to determine.

Monk and Ham knew it was the small sound which Doc Savage made in moments of intense mental activity.

Doc placed the wreck of the typewriter on the desk.

"This might interest you," he said.

Monk and Ham came over to look. Astonishment took them both with a jerk.

"Blazes!" Monk grunted.

"By Jove!" Ham exclaimed.

With the point of a pen, Monk lifted a strip of rubbery red substance from a sharp edge of the typewriter. He spread this out and worried it with the pen point until he had it made into an irregularly shaped ribbon. The color of the stuff was deep scarlet.

"It's a piece of hide," Monk muttered, *"off something red!"*

Doc and his aids peered at the piece of skin. Then they looked around the room some more. There were no more pieces of red hide.

"But there's bloodstains on the floor," Ham pointed out with his sword cane.

"It must have been some fight," Monk said wistfully. "I kinda wish I had been in it."

Next to quarreling with Ham and making love to a pretty girl, Monk liked a good fight best.

They went back to the piece of red hide.

"It ain't human hide," Monk announced in a queer voice. "It's got a different texture."

"Maybe it's only dyed red," Ham suggested.

Doc Savage made an examination with a powerful pocket magnifier.

"The pigmentation permeates the tissue," he remarked.

"You sound like Johnny," Monk complained. "What do you mean?"

"The skin does not seem to be dyed," Doc said.

"To sum this up," Monk said, "we know there was a fight and somebody threw a typewriter at *somethin'*, and a piece of the *somethin's* hide stuck to the typewriter."

"It's a pleasure to notice you have it clear in your mind," Ham said. "As usual, you're mixed up."

Doc Savage sprinkled dark fingerprint powder on the papers on the desk and put white powder on the furniture and desk. Then he blew away surplus powder and examined the prints through a pocket magnifier.

"There are three sets of recent fingerprints," he announced.

Monk said, "I've got a photostat of Doctor Collendar's fingerprints here. Got them from our information file on the fellow."

The homely chemist handed over a standard police fingerprint card, and Doc Savage compared this with the tent prints in the office.

"Doctor Collendar was in this office during the fight,"

the bronze man stated. "Here are his fingerprints where he apparently picked up the typewriter to throw it."

"That accounts for one set of fingerprints," Monk said. "What about the other two?"

The telephone was loose from its wires as if it had been used as a club in the fight. Doc Savage indicated the fingerprints of the person who had wielded the instrument.

"Notice something unusual about these?"

Monk peered through the magnifying glass. "Why, heck! These fingerprints ain't got no whorls or lines. They look like they'd been made by gloves. But gloves don't leave prints!"

"Those prints," Doc Savage said, "were probably made by someone who has had a plastic surgery operation to make identification by fingerprints impossible."

"I thought the whorls and lines always grew back on the finger tips after such operations," Monk said.

"Not at once. Fingerprint identification can be prevented for a year or two by that method."

"Crooks," Monk said, "are the only people who want their fingerprints wiped out. Maybe a crook swung the telephone."

"You're very bright today," Ham told Monk.

"What about the third and last set of fingerprints?" Monk asked.

"The third set," Doc said, "will have to be checked."

Doc photographed the third set of prints and sent them to the Department of Justice in Washington. Word came back that the prints were not on record there. The police of New York, Jersey City, Philadelphia, Boston and other cities did not have the prints on file.

The next day, the fingerprints were found in the files of the American Union of Deep-Sea Divers. The prints belonged to a diver named Harry Day.

After he had made some inquiries about Harry Day, Monk came into Doc's headquarters looking queer.

"This Harry Day," Monk gulped, "was on a ship that sank in mid-Atlantic several months ago!"

Ham peered at Monk. "Are you crazy?"

"I ain't as sure about it as I was last week," Monk confessed.

Doc Savage did not seem concerned, surprised or

particularly impressed by the news. This did not surprise Monk and Ham; they had known the bronze man for years, and they had never got over being startled by the control he could exercise over himself. He must be impressed by what had happened, but he did not show it.

Two men had drowned near the same spot in the Atlantic Ocean, several months apart. Now the two men had turned up in New York. This should be enough to impress anybody, including Doc Savage, who was perfectly human.

The bronze man had all the usual human qualities, in spite of the fact that he had been trained so intensively and scientifically that he was a physical marvel and a mental genius.

Later Renny, the big-fisted engineer, came in. The sad look on his long face did not mean a thing, being the expression he wore from habit.

"Holy cow!" Renny grumbled. "No luck at all."

"What have you been doing?" Monk wanted to know.

"Trying to find some trace of Doctor Collendar," Renny said.

"Doctor Collendar's associates think he drowned. They think you're crazy when you ask 'em if they've seen Doctor Collendar the last day or two."

The rumble of Renny's voice usually caused listeners to look instinctively to see if the walls were shaking.

Long Tom Roberts and Johnny Littlejohn came into the office and informed Doc they had found no trace of a man named Snig Bogaccio.

"Who in blazes is Snig Bogaccio?" Monk inquired.

"A maleficiently iniquitous anthropogenical specimen," Johnny replied.

"Huh?"

"A gangster," Long Tom translated.

"Why couldn't he say so," Monk complained, "Instead of dishing out them alphabetical *hors d'oeuvres* he calls English language."

Ham added, "And what has a gangster named Snig Bogaccio got to do with this mystery?"

"Well, the police think Doctor Collendar performed a plastic surgery operation on Snig Bogaccio."

Monk snapped his fingers. "Hey! In Doctor Collendar's

office, we found fingerprints left by somebody who'd had a plastic surgery operation!"

"We also found some red hide off *something!*" Ham said.

"Depend on you to drag a polecat into the discussion," Monk grumbled.

Chapter V

THE HIDING DIVER

Doc Savage went away unobtrusively for a few minutes and made some telephone calls to the company which handled insurance for the divers' union, inquiring about Harry Day's family. Then he rejoined his five assistants.

"Harry Day, the deep-sea diver, has a sister," the bronze man said.

"Is she good-lookin'?" Monk asked.

"The sister's name is Edwina Day, and she lives in an apartment on Central Park West," Doc Savage added. "We can pay her a visit and see if she can tell us anything about her brother."

"I'll bet she's a blonde," Monk said, "and as cute as a pickle seed."

Edwina Day was not a blonde. She was Spanish-dark, and she was small. But she was conceivably as cute as a pickle seed, a pickle seed being an elastic yardstick for measuring feminine beauty. The reception she gave them was also somewhat picklish.

"Whatever you are selling, I don't want any," she said, looking at them like a startled bird.

27

"Wait a minute," Monk said. "This is about your brother!"

He evidently said the wrong thing, because the girl tried to slam the door in their faces. Renny got a big fist in the way of the door.

"Mayn't we come in?" Renny rumbled politely.

"No!" the girl gritted. "Get away from here! All of you!"

Renny shoved against the door, pushed door and girl back, and they all marched in gravely.

"I'll call the police!" the young woman threatened.

"Isn't there enough of them in here now to suit you?" Renny asked.

"You aren't policemen!"

"We've got commissions," Renny explained. "I was under the impression they made you a cop." Doc Savage and his five men held honorary commissions which did make them, technically, officers.

"Oh!" The girl frosted them with her stare. "I might have guessed you were policemen."

The madder Edwina Day became, the cuter Monk thought she looked.

"This is Doc Savage." Monk indicated Doc.

This information usually had an effect.

"He'll be Doctor Mild-as-watered-milk if he doesn't get out of here!" the girl said.

Monk gathered that she had never heard of Doc Savage, or wasn't impressed.

"We seek information," Monk explained.

"What you'll get," the girl said, "is air." She looked them over. "Some collection of freaks," she added.

"Ain't you never heard of us?" Monk demanded incredulously.

"You should get a tent," the young woman remarked, "and charge admissions." She considered. "Two cents would be a fair price."

Long Tom said, "Now look here, Miss Day, we merely came to see you because we have—"

"Thank you, and I don't want any," interrupted the girl. "It's nice to have met you. Good afternoon! Get out!"

"—we have a problem," Long Tom continued. "Your brother, Harry Day, is supposed to have drowned months ago. And now he seems to be mixed up in a fight with something red—"

The girl jumped.

"*What!*"

Long Tom said, "That's the rub. We don't know what."

The girl took a tight handful of her frock over her breasts with her right hand, took a handful of her left cheek with her left hand, and began to walk backward.

Ham said in uneasy apology, "I'm awfully sorry we barged in here like this."

Monk, not to be outdone, added, "If it frightens you so, we'll leave."

Big-fisted, sad-faced Renny, as romantic as a chew of tobacco, said, "Like blazes we'll leave! There's somethin' wrong here!" He took a step forward. "What do you know about this red stuff? What in the name of holy cows is this all about?"

The girl began to shake.

"You say—my brother—something red?" She was incoherent.

Renny frowned. "I see you know somethin' about it!"

The girl looked at the floor. Her eyes selected a spot and focused, and she fell toward the spot, stiff and unbending, falling as a tree falls.

Monk and Ham jumped for her simultaneously, collided with each other, and looked foolish. The girl thumped the floor.

"She's dead!" Monk croaked.

"She must have had a weak heart!" Ham groaned. "We shouldn't have cut down on her like that."

Bony Johnny got down on his knees beside the girl and held one of her wrists with a hand that shook until he could hardly hold the wrist. Then he looked sheepish.

"Syncopic lipothymy," he muttered.

"Eh?" Monk looked puzzled.

"He means she just throwed a Joe," Long Tom said.

"Try English," Monk requested.

"She fainted!" Ham squatted by the girl. "I'll rub her wrists until—"

Doc Savage said, "Our best move is to get out of here."

"But Doc—"

The bronze man made a slight gesture. Without more objections, his associates followed him out of the apartment.

Monk and the others had learned it was unwise to argue with Doc. Not that he had any rules against arguments. He didn't. It was simply that his batting average on judgment was so high that it was pretty dependable.

Monk complained. "We shouldn't have left her lyin' there in a faint—"

"She was faking the faint," Doc said, "to keep us from questioning her."

When the elevator came for them, Doc Savage seized the control and ran the car straight to the basement, disregarding astonished glares from other passengers. He whipped across the basement to the telephone connector box, yanked it open, and examined the labels alongside the maze of binding posts. He clipped a line-tapping receiver onto the wire to Edwina Day's apartment.

Half a dozen loud clicks, unevenly spaced, came out of the receiver.

"We cut in as she finished dialing a number!" Monk groaned.

"And too late to learn the number from the clicks," Ham added.

Doc Savage used a pocketknife to span binding posts and make a short circuit, creating the same effect as if the girl had hung up her receiver. The connection which she had set up by dialing was broken.

"Hello," the girl said. "Hello . . . hello!" A moment later: "Oh, darn!"

She had to dial again. Doc listened to the clicking of the dial mechanism with the experienced ear of a telegraph operator trained to counting dots.

"She called Sand Hills 9-3312," Doc said. "Long Tom, you get the location from the telephone company."

The anemic-looking electrical wizard hurried off.

Doc listened, and a voice said, "The Palace Barber Shop."

It was a man's voice.

The girl said, "Harry!" wildly.

"Edwina!" the man said. "What's wrong? Collendar may have this line tapped! I told you not to call!"

"Oh, Harry!" Agitation made the girl's voice hoarse. "A bunch of men were just here!"

The man made a gutteral, frantic noise.

"Collendar!" he barked.

Monk, listening over Doc's shoulder, looked stunned.

"Harry Day must be alive, too!" he croaked.

The girl's voice said, "Harry these men said they were with someone called Doc Savage. Does Collendar use the name of Savage sometimes?"

Harry Day yelled, *"Doc Savage?"*

"Yes."

Harry Day clucked disgustedly.

"I'm a damn fool not to have thought of Doc Savage before this!" he shouted.

"What do you mean?"

"Even in Africa, I heard talk of Doc Savage. But it never entered my thick head to call on him for help."

"Maybe this man wasn't Doc Savage."

"What'd he look like?"

"A giant. But he didn't seem so large until you got close—"

"That's him! Look, sis! Get hold of Savage! Or learn where I can talk to him by telephone."

"You—"

"I want to talk to Doc Savage!" Harry Day shouted.

The silence that followed was long enough for the girl to do some intent thinking.

"Harry," she said queerly.

"Well, what is it?"

"Harry, I—well, won't you go to a psychiatrist?" The girl sounded as if she had been biting holes in her tongue.

Harry Day swore, swore a trifle wildly, as though he were in a very dark room and wasn't sure but that there might be a something hungry and man-eating in the room. He swore as if trying to keep up his courage in that room. He stopped swearing.

"I'm not crazy!" he said.

The girl began to talk like a woman telling a boy it was better to pull a tooth out than to let it ache.

"A person can experience hallucinations without being insane, Harry," she said earnestly. "A profound shock can cause delirium. You received a shock when the steamer *Muddy Mary* sank."

"Oh, hell! I'm not crazy!"

"You might have been struck on the head by wreckage or something."

"Some of my boxed equipment rolled on me as the ship sank," Harry Day admitted. "But I tell you that—"

"You may have been in a coma afterward. You could have imagined things. Perhaps a ship picked you up."

"I tell you—"

"Harry!" the girl said firmly. "Probably you only imagined what you think happened. *You had to imagine it!*"

Doc Savage was motionless and intent at the listen-in receiver.

Long Tom came back and said, "I've got the address."

The bronze man moved a finger for silence.

"I didn't imagine anything!" Harry screamed. "The steamer sank with me in her hold almost a year ago!" He took in a windy breath. "I've told you everything that happened after that, and God knows I don't blame you for thinking I'm crazy."

The girl's sigh was defeat.

"I'll try to get hold of Doc Savage," she promised.

"I'll wait for your call."

Clickings broke the telephone connection. Big-fisted Renny pulled his mouth corners down thoughtfully. "Holy cow! This Harry Day has been through something so strange he thinks he did imagine it!"

Doc Savage asked, "Where was Harry Day talking from?"

Long Tom said, "No. 11 Conkley Street."

"Monk, Ham and myself will go after Harry Day," Doc said. "Renny, Long Tom and Johnny get hold of the girl. Harry Day has told her his story. Get her to repeat it."

"Ah, bugs!" Monk said.

"Something wrong?" Ham inquired.

"Doc is kinda overlookin' my power over women," Monk said.

Ham snorted.

"What Doc isn't overlooking," said the dapper lawyer unkindly, "is the power of women over you!"

Chapter VI

THE VANISHING MEN

Conkley Street did not appeal to Monk. He gave it a long look.

"Phooey!" he said.

Ham chuckled. "Nothing would look good to you right now."

"That girl would." Monk pulled the ear of his pet pig ecstatically. "Oh, boy, was she a morsel! I always did like them small and dark."

Doc Savage was silent, his flake gold eyes fixed on long horns of light that stuck out of the headlamps. The sun had gone away and left blackness and low clouds. The clouds were leaking a few raindrops that burst on the windshield like fat, transparent bugs. The windshield wipers rocked back and forth lazily.

Monk heaved a sigh. "Granting that she's a pretty girl—which we will—this is still a very mythogenic situation."

"A which?" Ham asked, scratching Chemistry's head.

"I got that word from Johnny," Monk explained.

'Mythogenic—meaning a business that is kinda hard to believe."

Ham frowned at Monk. "I've got it!"

"Got what?"

"Your number. You're mythogenic yourself."

"How do you figure that?"

"When people look at you the first time," Ham said, "they always find it hard to believe the human race produced you."

Conkley Street took another turn. It had already taken several turns in dodging the seashore. Wet mutter of breaking waves could be heard when rain was not slopping on the car, and salt of the sea was in the damp air almost enough to taste.

Wind had blown yellow beach sand across the pavement in drifts, and automobile tracks in the drifts were scarce enough to indicate there was not much traffic on Conkley Street.

Bungalows on Conkley Street got more blowsy. The first ones had been as neat as girls in graduation dresses. Now they dirtied up and lost their paint, became slatterns, scarecrow frameworks dressed in canvas which wind had tattered and sun had turned a dead-rat color that sun gives canvas.

At No. 11, the car turned in and its headlights washed whitely over a bungalow that was something that looked as though it might have been through a plague of moths.

"A kind of cheesy joint," Monk suggested.

"You're right, you mythogenic," Ham said.

Ham suddenly bolted upright, grabbed Doc's arm and pointed.

"Look at that!"

Window curtains of the bungalow were drawn, and a man with a gun stood between the curtain and a light. He was nearer the light and his shadow on the curtain was magnified. The automatic he held was a big thing with a barrel like a piece sawed off a walking stick.

The gun and hand began to jerk around. Shot sounds came out of the bungalow. It sounded as if a huge hammer had started beating the walls.

The man with the gun must have been shooting at several targets, because he was crouching and turning as he fired, raking the room behind the window. The shadow of the gun showed that it was equipped with a ram-horn magazine.

Then something from behind sprang upon the man with the gun. The shadows were too confused to identify the thing that leaped upon the man.

Doc Savage gave the engine gas. The machine bucked over the curbing. Rocking and skidding, wheels throwing sand, the machine circled the house. The dashboard was equipped with a surplus of levers and knobs. Doc Savage held a thumb on one of the knobs; there was a loud hissing, and bluish vapor poured from under the car.

Doc drove completely around the house twice, took his thumb off the knob, and tanks under the car ceased spewing gas. He stopped the car.

"Give that gas five minutes!" the bronze man said.

Wind came in off the sea, caught the gas, pushed it into the bungalow through open windows and doors. The gas whirled like cigarette smoke in the car's headlights, surrounded the car.

Monk said, "I hope Renny did a good job when he gave this car its last gas test."

Big-fisted Renny saw to the construction and maintenance of their mechanical equipment.

Ham fiddled nervously with his sword cane. "Doc, did you see what jumped on the man with the gun?"

"Only the shadow of it."

"What was it?"

The bronze man looked at Ham, and suddenly his weird, trilling sound was in the car. As always, it rose and fell with a definite musical quality, but now it also had an excited vibrance that was new to the sound.

Ham said, *"The thing that jumped wasn't a man!"*

Monk snorted, "Don't be silly! It had to be a man!"

"You mythogenic!" Ham said. "It wasn't a man!"

"It must have been a gollywockus," Monk suggested.

"We have given the gas enough time. It has been absorbed by the air by now and is harmless," Doc Savage said.

Each man carried a flashlight in his left hand, and Monk and Ham carried machine-pistols in their right hands. The machine-pistols, little larger than automatics, could fire fast enough to sound like big bullfiddles, and were charged with "mercy" bullets, which produced unconsciousness only.

Doc, Monk and Ham piled out of the car, ran to the bungalow, leaving the pets in the car. The door was open. They went in, flashlights spiking white.

First came a front room, absolutely naked, beach sand on the floor. There was a door straight ahead and one to the right.

Monk, always impulsive in a fight, shouldered hard on the door to the right. It caved. Monk went plunging in and rooted a closet wall. He backed out, looking foolish.

"Typical of a mythogenic," Ham told him.

Doc Savage went at the other door, right arm rigid ready to hit. The lock splintered out and the door flew back, and they charged into another naked room.

A kitchen next. Then a bedroom on the right, another bedroom left. The kitchen had a pantry. Both bedrooms had closets. Rooms, pantries, closets were empty.

Monk spotted a hatch leading into the attic. Monk sprang a prodigious height for such a short fellow, and knocked a lid away, sprang again, chinned himself, scanned the attic with his flashlight beam.

"Heck!" he said, and dropped back. Then he ran through rooms looking at the floors, but there was no basement door.

"Great ghosts!" Monk exploded. "We saw a man here, but he ain't here now."

"He's got to be!" Ham snapped.

"Maybe you see 'im!" Monk growled.

Whenever they moved their feet on the floor, sand rasped and groaned, so they did not move their feet any more than they had to. The place was spooky. Wind pushed against the bungalow and made it creak, and occasional raindrops landing on walls or roof sounded like big mice running senselessly.

"Spooky place!" Monk gulped.

Ham said, "Any place'd be spooky after what happened!"

Doc Savage had been listening. For two hours each day he performed exercises which had given him the agile mind and almost incredible physical strength which he possessed. This scientific training had given him hearing faculties beyond the ordinary. So he caught sounds that the others missed.

"Something happening on the beach," he said abruptly.

They raced out of the bungalow and followed the beams of their flashlights toward the sea. Sand dunes shouldered up around them. Sand soon got deep enough to fill their trousers cuffs.

Monk turned his flashlight beam aside at an object in the sand and yelled, "There's the gun!"

Doc Savage had seen the weapon. It was a spiked-nose automatic with a ram-horn magazine.

The others now heard the sounds from the beach. Cries. A man screeching in fear.

The man who was crying out was in the sea twenty yards or so out. Half of him was above the water, and he was throwing blow after blow at something under him. Waves hid whatever the man was fighting.

The man was very tall, and his hair was white and stood up to give the effect of an Indian with a headdress of white feathers.

"Harry Day!" Monk yelled. "That's Harry Day!"

A wave fell on Harry Day and covered him and whatever it was that was dragging him into the sea. More waves, coming in and piling up in the shoal water, made breakers as high as the man's shoulder. Harry Day did not appear again.

"Keep your lights on the water," Doc ordered.

Going into the sea, the bronze man dived sideways through the breakers. Brilliance from the flashlights held by Monk and Ham on shore turned the wave crests into white masses, and wave hollows were squirming black, and all around was water noise. Doc Savage swam and hunted for nearly fifteen minutes.

"No trace!" he said, coming back.

"Come over here, Doc," Ham muttered. "Look at the trail the thing made dragging Harry Day."

The trail was a pocked hodgepodge in the sand. Doc Savage began at the water and followed it back to the bungalow, taking pains. Nowhere did he find a footprint which seemed to belong to a man. They were just pits in the sand.

Monk said, "They *could* have been men! Notice the kind of footprints we're makin'. It ain't rained enough to soak the sand. Wet sand on top sticks to our shoes and we just leave marks when we walk."

Doc Savage recovered the automatic pistol they had seen. The ram-horn magazine was half empty. He carried the weapon inside the bungalow, dried it carefully, and found fingerprints.

"Let's have the card with Harry Day's prints." He compared the card with the gun prints, then said, "Harry Day used this gun."

Monk went over the bungalow floors and examined bullet pits in the walls. He dug out a slug or two.

"There ain't no bloodstains where nothin' was hit," he complained.

Doc Savage went out to the car and turned on the short-wave radio, let the tubes warm, and cut in the microphone.

When his men worked separately from the bronze man, it was their custom to keep a short-wave receiver cut in on the wave length they used.

"Long Tom!"

"Yes, Doc?" Long Tom's voice said.

"You get the girl?"

"Yes. We're not makin' headway, though."

"Where are you?"

"Her apartment."

"Will she talk?"

"She talks plenty," Long Tom said. "But not what we want to hear."

Doc Savage said, "Harry Day was seized by *something*, and carried into the sea."

"*Something?*" Long Tom exploded. "What do you mean?"

"Keep a close watch on the girl," Doc Savage directed. "We'll join you."

"O.K., Doc."

Chapter VII

THE HOSPITAL RAIDERS

Long Tom comtemplated his short-wave radio transceiver approvingly. The device—his own invention—was hardly larger than a folding pocket Kodak, and reliable within horizon range. Batteries, antenna were self-contained, and a buzzer sounded whenever another station called.

"Get out of here!" Edwina Day ordered. "All three of you!"

Long Tom ignored her. "Monk and Ham and Doc are coming up."

"What do you clowns think this'll get you?" the girl complained.

Big-fisted Renny gave her a long face. "Plenty, my fire-cracker female. Several months ago your brother was on a ship that sank in the Atlantic. There was a diphtheria plague on the ship. All hands and passengers supposedly drowned."

The girl chewed the inside of her mouth and said nothing.

Renny boomed, "Now your brother turns up in New

York. Doctor Collendar, another man who disappeared in the Atlantic, turns up, too. Also something red, of which nobody has seen enough to know what it is."

The girl suddenly sat down loosely in a chair.

Renny thumped. "And now your brother Harry has been dragged into the ocean."

The girl came up rigid, staring, and her mouth made words, but her throat would not make the sounds to go with them. Her fingers dug handfuls of air.

"They took—Harry—"

Renny was no diplomat, and now seemed a good time to shock the girl into talking. He said, "If you'd talked instead of givin' us sass, maybe we could've stopped it."

The word blast was effective. The girl's fingers stopped working and balled into tight fists. "Who told you my brother had been—taken?"

"Doc Savage."

"Did he see it happen?"

"From the way Doc talked, think he did."

Edwina Day made a strangled sound. "And I thought Harry was insane!"

Renny said, "Give us your brother's story."

The girl appeared not to hear him. Her eyes had an expression of peering into distances.

Johnny broke the stillness with a roar. He rarely roared. And when he followed the roar with words, they were very short words.

"The window!" he squalled.

The girl looked at the window. She screamed as if trying to take the lining out of her throat, kept on screaming and pitched to the door, yanked it open, dived into the corridor. But the next instant she was back in the apartment, still screaming.

"Hall full of them!" she screeched.

Then the lights went out, and a moment later the apartment was full of blackness and struggle.

A large, neat policeman stopped Doc Savage's sedan a block from Edwina Day's apartment house, said, "No traffic on this street for a while." Then he saw Doc Savage behind the wheel. "Oh, I beg pardon."

There were policemen, police cars, and people in the street ahead, and a white ambulance or two.

"What has happened?" Doc asked.

"Nobody seems to know," the cop said. "Some kind of riot. Lights went out."

Doc Savage drove on. Ham's hands were tight on his sword cane. "I don't like this," he said.

The sedan had colored police headlights and regulation siren, and Doc turned the light on, moaned the siren softly until they stopped in front of Edwina Day's tall apartment building.

There was a crowd around the entrance. A man in the crowd said, "They're bringin' the fellow out now!"

After a commotion in the lobby, white-coated internes, carrying a stretcher and surrounded by policemen, appeared.

"Johnny!" Monk squalled.

Johnny was string-limp on the stretcher. His eyes were open.

"Johnny!" Monk roared. "Are you hurt bad?"

"Sort of superamalgamated!" Johnny managed.

Doc said, "We'll take charge of him," to the stretcher attendants. The bronze man began an examination.

Despite the dark night, no street lamps were lighted in the neighborhood. Nor were there lights in windows. The only light came from flashlights of policemen, and big floodlights on police emergency trucks.

Rain was sifting down and the drops glistened like jewels in the floodlights.

Doc asked, "What did this to you?"

Johnny said, "I don't know."

"You don't know?"

"We were in the girl's apartment," Johnny said. "After that, it's hazy. The lights went out." He closed his eyes and winced. "I was hit a lot of times."

"What hit you?"

Johnny squeezed his eyelids together. "I couldn't tell much."

"What did they *feel* like?"

"Hard," Johnny muttered. "Harder than flesh would feel. It was so infernally dark."

Monk said, "Is he hurt bad, Doc? He sounds delirious."

"An arm and both legs broken," the bronze man said. "Maybe more."

Monk asked, "What became of Renny and Long Tom?"

"I do not know," Johnny said. "I never saw them after I went out the window."

"Went out the window?"

Johnny explained, "I was standing in front of a window when something hit me."

An ambulance man volunteered, "They found him in the concrete courtyard in the back."

Doc Savage went into the building and searched Edwina Day's apartment, then searched all the other apartments. He found no trace of Renny, Long Tom, the girl —nor any trace of the mysterious assailants who had attacked his men.

Doc Savage and the police learned several things. Two large moving vans had backed up to the apartment house before the attack. The vans left immediately following the attack. An operator had been on duty at the elevator and had seen the van back up and gone out to ask questions.

Doc found the operator where he had been dropped behind some ash cans, revived him, and got his story. He had been hit with a Stillson wrench. The vans had been yellow. But his descriptions of vans and drivers were not explicit enough to help much.

Light company men learned what had cut off electricity to the neighborhood. Someone had taken an ax to the mains. They found the ax, partly eaten by electricity. The ax handle had been wound with insulating tape.

Black stickum from the tape had stuck to the ax wielder's fingers, and they found his fingerprints. They were the fingerprints of a man who had had a plastic surgery operation on his finger tips.

"Same prints as in Collendar's office," Monk remarked.

"For a mythogenic, you've got good memory," Ham offered.

Doc Savage said nothing. Monk and Ham could see that he was worried. They accompanied the bronze man to Research Hospital, where Doc worked over Johnny, X-raying, diagnosing and treating. He spent nearly two hours in doing what he could for Johnny.

"Lucky to be alive," the bronze man said grimly.

In working on Johnny, Doc Savage used an operating room which was encircled by a glassed-in balcony. The balcony was crowded with surgeons and doctors who had rushed there to watch the bronze man work.

Doc Savage was skilled in many professions, but his reputation as a surgeon probably exceeded all others. Monk and Ham paced the balcony, so nervously that they drew irritated glares.

"I'm plenty worried about Renny and Long Tom," Monk groaned.

Ham said, "What could've happened to them?"

The question was answered partly the next morning, when the telephone rang in Doc Savage's skyscraper headquarters. An operative in the bronze man's private detective agency was on the wire.

"Think we've located the vans."

"Where?" Doc asked.

"A warehouse in Brooklyn." He gave the address.

The warehouse stood behind a careening wooden fence. It was an ancient pile in a part of Brooklyn that had gone to seed.

The vans were large, yellow. The interiors had been given a thorough scrubbing with soap and water. Soap brushes and buckets containing soapy water stood behind the van.

"Good-by, fingerprints!" Monk said.

Doc Savage said, "Test it for chalk."

For a long time, the bronze man and his aids had utilized for secret communications a chalk which left a mark invisible to the naked eye, but which fluoresced or glowed under ultraviolet light. The invisible chalk could not be removed readily by scrubbing. Certain buttons on the garments which Doc and his men wore were composed of the stuff.

Doc switched on one of the tiny lanterns which they employed to project ultraviolet lights. The device somewhat resembled an old-fashioned magic-lantern with a blue-black lens. They searched the van interior carefully with ultraviolet light.

The message on the van floor said:

WATCH RESEARCH HOSPITAL

That was all that had been written.

"Renny's handwritin'!" Monk said.

They decided that Renny had been caught writing the message and whoever had caught him had stamped on the chalk. There was a smear of the stuff at the end of the message.

Ham pointed at the message with his sword cane. "Doesn't make sense."

"Neither does this whole mess!" Monk grumbled.

Doc Savage said, "We will watch Research Hospital."

Research Hospital was justification for an economic system which permits men to make billion-dollar fortunes. For if one man had not made a billion, Research Hospital might never have come into existence, and quite a few thousand people would have died as an indirect result.

For the serum developed by scientists on the staff of Research Hospital had saved quite a few thousand lives. The institution was world renowned as a serum source. It was an impressive array of brick-walled towers. The buildings alone had cost a hundred million dollars.

Arrival of Doc Savage created a stir, for the bronze man had helped design the hospital, and was on its board of scientific research. Hoping that Renny, Long Tom and the girl might have been brought to the hospital as emergency cases, Doc Savage checked over the recently admitted patients. Nothing there.

"Blast it," Monk said. "Why'd Renny want us to watch the place?"

"If they hadn't caught Renny leaving the note!" Ham groaned.

Because Research Hospital was the only clue they had. Doc Savage and his men could only keep vigil at the institution.

By the next day Johnny had improved enough to talk more coherently. But he added nothing to what he had said earlier. The raid on Edwina Day's apartment had been spectral and violent, and Johnny had been knocked backward out of the window before he had really learned anything.

"An imperspicuous oppugnancy!" Johnny remarked.

"He must be gettin' better," Monk remarked, "but what'd he say?"

"Said it was puzzling," Ham translated.

"I didn't know you could speak his language," Monk grunted. "Tell him he said a mouthful."

It was ten minutes past midnight when a buzzer squealed in the hospital office. Doc Savage turned from a table on which he had been sketching and explaining a method of treating the part of the human brain known as the mesial accessory olivary nucleus. The squealing buzzer was attached to the hospital fire alarm.

Doc Savage joined a rush for the annunciator which would show the location of the fire. The bronze man's face was grim; fires in hospitals can be pretty terrible things.

"In the serum vaults!" an attendant barked.

The array of serum vaults was one of the remarkable features of Research Hospital. Serum manufactured by the staff of scientists was kept there. The vaults were very large, containing a supply from which serum was shipped to most parts of the world.

The vaults were divided into sections according to the temperature at which they were maintained. Some of the serum and germ cultures had to be kept near boiling temperature, and the others were kept at various degrees of coolness.

Doc led the rush from the annunciator board to the vaults. There was a long white corridor off which the serum compartments opened. In the corridor, an attendant, who was an undersized collection of wrinkles, was jumping up and down, pawing at his eyes and howling.

"Fire's in the diptheria vault!" someone shouted.

The vault doors looked like the doors in butcher shop refrigerators. Over the one marked "Diphtheria Antitoxin" an electric bulb glowed red.

News that the blaze was in the diphtheria compartment had an unusual effect on the bronze man. He came to a stop. His trilling sound was audible for a startled moment. Then his big frame was blocking the others from the corridor.

"Ham," Doc called, "get a telephone and have police surround the hospital. Stop everything!"

"Right!" Ham was gone.

Monk grabbed the wrinkled attendant, and peered closely at him.

Monk said, "Blazes, Doc! This guy's got somethin' wrong with 'im!"

"Tear gas," Doc Savage said. To the men he was keeping from the vault corridor, Doc said, "If you want to be safe, get away from this part of the building."

"But—"

"This is more than a fire," Doc said. "Get back!"

There was such an impelling power in the crash of his voice that the men withdrew. Monk meantime shook the shriveled attendant and yelled, "Where'd you get the tear gas?"

The man coughed, sneezed, said, "In the vault." He beat his chest and clutched his throat. "Somethin' in there!"

Monk looked dumfounded. "Huh?"

"Somebody in a red coat!" the attendant wailed.

From his carry-all vest, Doc Savage took nose clips, a breath-filter, and goggles with mechanically intricate lenses as large as condensed milk cans. He put on the clips and snapped the goggles over his eyes. Then he produced a fistful of smoke bombs of his own design and a lamp which projected strong infrared rays slightly outside the visible spectrum.

Monk equipped himself likewise, and grinned. Prospects of a fracas always exhilarated Monk.

Doc Savage opened the vault door and stepped into the heat-insulating lock. Ten feet distant was another door of the lock. Doc opened it. Both doors were almost a foot thick.

The interior of the diphtheria vault was very dark.

The bronze man heaved half a dozen smoke bombs which made loud hissing noises and spewed black vapor.

The goggles which Doc and Monk wore had been perfected by the bronze man and utilized a chemical concoction sensitive to infrared light. The infra light would penetrate smoke and fog far better than ordinary light. The images seen in the mechanical goggles differed from pictures ordinarily seen by the eye in that they were semi-luminous.

Doc and Monk entered the vault.

There was a man in the vault. The man wore a hood-type gas mask, carried a gun in his right hand, and his left hand held a suitcase gorged with small packets of diphtheria antitoxin. The man was backing nervously toward a hole which had been opened in the vault wall, He could not see a thing in the smoke.

The vault must have been approached from the outside by tunneling, and a cutting torch used to make a hole in the steel wall; the torch had probably set fire to wooden shelves on which antitoxin was racked.

Doc Savage attacked from the side, seized the man's gun, squeezed, and the victim's shrieks were piercing, even through his gas mask. Monk came in and would have knocked the fellow unconscious had Doc not blocked the blow. Doc twisted until he secured the gun, then shoved the captive to Monk to hold.

Getting down on hands and knees, Doc Savage crawled through the hole in the side of the vault into a tunnel three feet high and not quite as wide. Floor and walls were dirt; planks shored up the roof. The tunnel ran straight, and from its length and direction, obviously was passing under the street.

Doc crawled out of the tunnel into a basement where there were heaps of dirt and another man.

The man was across the room. When he saw Doc, he jumped back through a door and slammed the door; he had it locked by the time Doc reached it. It was a heavy door.

Doc inserted a high-explosive cartridge in the lock and put a match to the fuse. The cartridge resembled the firecrackers which come in nickel packages, and it blew about half of the wooden door into splinters.

Doc went through, climbed a stairway into a house, bounded across rooms, and reached the street in time to see a car leaving.

The car was stacked with diphtheria antitoxin containers.

Doc found a telephone and gave the car license numbers to the police. Then he went back to the hospital.

Chapter VIII

THE SECOND RESURRECTION

Monk had taken the prisoner to a private room. Monk was threatening to knock out the captive's teeth, and break off his fingers, then pull out his eyeballs and let them snap back again if he did not talk.

The prisoner sneered at these threats.

"He's kinda tough, Doc," Monk said.

The prisoner looked at Doc Savage and underwent a change. He muttered, "I figured you was kiddin' when you said you was one of the bronze guy's outfit."

Doc Savage went into another room where he had some of his equipment and came back adjusting the point in a hypodermic needle.

The prisoner, who was lashed wrist and ankle with adhesive tape, stared at Doc Savage. His eyes popped and the corners of his mouth began to leak saliva.

"What're you gonna do?" he croaked.

Monk looked as fierce as he could.

"One shot of that stuff," the homely chemist growled untruthfully, "and for the rest of their lives they can't move, talk or do nothin' a-tall."

The prisoner had a convulsion and courage jumped out of him. "Don't do it!" he squawled. "Maybe we can make a deal!"

"We do not make deals," Doc Savage said.

The bronze man emptied the contents of the hypodermic needle into the victim. It was truth serum.

Approximately twenty minutes were required for the truth serum to reach maximum effects where the victim's faculties were dulled, and blankness of his eyes and stupid looseness of his face indicated that his control over himself was nullified. The suppression extended to the man's vocal chords, making him talk like a man who was extremely drunk. Doc Savage asked questions and got answers.

The prisoner was Ted Malarkio. He was a safecracker. He had been approached by Harry Day, the deep-sea diver.

Doc Savage asked, "What did Harry Day hire you to do?"

"He wansh dissherry sherrum," the man said thickly.

"Harry Day hired you to steal the serum?"

The safe-breaker said this was right.

"But if Day wanted serum, why not buy it?" homely Monk interrupted.

Doc Savage explained. "Some antitoxins are poisonous," the bronze man said, "and some are cultures of germs. Recently, it was discovered that a European power at war was buying germs to use on the enemy. Since then, all purchases of antitoxin of germ culture have been checked thoroughly."

Monk said, "Then if anybody wanted a lot of serum and no questions asked, they'd have to steal it."

"That," Doc said, "is why they stole antitoxin."

Monk leaned close to the prisoner.

"Notice anything queer about Harry Day?"

The man mumbled something. Monk decided the fellow had noticed Harry Day seemed to be nervous about something. Monk wasn't satisfied. He demanded, "Ever see anything *red?*"

This question had such an effect on the captive that even Doc was startled. Monk's query must have delivered a profound shock, because the captive actually threw off the stupefying effects of the truth serum to a degree.

"Whash was it?" he croaked.

"What was what?" Monk asked.

"Thash blood-colored thing."

"If you saw it," Monk said, "you should know what it was."

The man shook his head vacantly. "Didn't get enough look to tell. Shaw it in Harry Day's bungalow."

Monk said, "Did Harry Day know the thing was there?"

"Sheemed to."

The prisoner grimaced, trying to draw his faculties together. The puckering effort showed on his face. He said, "Day didn't drown yesserday."

"He was mighty waterproof if he didn't," Monk grunted.

"I talked to Harry Day today!" the captive croaked. "Not more'n four hours ago."

Monk evidently had a great deal on his mind, but all he did was open and shut his mouth.

A police officer came in. "We threw a cordon around the hospital, as you suggested," he told Doc.

"What happened?"

"One car broke through." The officer scowled. "The back of the car was piled full of stuff."

"Diphtheria antitoxin," Doc said.

Monk held his head.

"Why'd they steal diphtheria antitoxin?" he demanded. "That's what gets me."

Their prisoner apparently decided to go whole hog in his confession.

"I was hired," he said. "I've been trying to go straight. Honest to blazes I have."

"That remark," Monk said, "is so old it has a long, flowing white beard."

"It may sound like a damn lie, but it's the truth," the captive insisted. "If you were paid what I was paid, you'd do it, too. Anyway, stealin' antitoxin ain't like stealin' money."

"How much you get paid?" Monk demanded.

The prisoner was mentally intoxicated by the truth

serum, and like an alcoholic drunk he wanted to prove that he was right.

"If you knew what I got for doin' it," he argued stupidly, "you'd do it, too."

"What'd you get?"

"At my room at the Gaine Hotel, in the closet wall—" The man stopped. He began to realize he had told too much.

Doc Savage asked, "Where were you to take the diphtheria antitoxin?"

The man was anxious to talk about something besides his hotel room. "To a steamer named the *Sea Mist*," he explained.

He didn't want them to go to his room! He wanted them to investigate the *Sea Mist*. He was as eager as a bird faking a broken wing to decoy a boy from its nest.

Doc Savage said, "Monk and Ham, you take this fellow and search his room."

The New York harbor master was pleasant enough when Doc Savage hurried into his office.

"The *Sea Mist*?" he said. "She's a banana hooker. Skipper owns her, I think." The harbor master frowned. "There was some talk of her shipping guns into Nicaragua and Cuba a few years ago."

"What part of the harbor is she lying?"

"Crummy little wharf near Backett Street."

The wharf was dilapidated enough, and the south side of it had caved in. However, there was a watchman in the little shack at the shoreward end.

"The *Sea Mist*?" the watchman said. "She high-tailed it forty-five minutes ago." The watchman chewed his lower lip sourly. "Funny business, if you ask me."

"Funny business?"

"A car come hell-bent for election and unloaded stuff. Then they sailed." The watchman scratched the back of his neck.

"Then there was them yellow vans. They backed up to the steamer a few nights ago and unloaded somethin'. Think I saw some people tied up with ropes. Then they saw me watchin'. Told me to vamoose." The watchman spat. "Right tough they was, too."

"See the prisoners?"

"Not close. One skinny 'un, though."

"Did they load cargo?" Doc inquired.

"Not much. What they did load was small boxes and heavy." The watchman scowled. "Guns in the boxes."

"Guns?"

"Hell, yes! Guns!" The watchman pointed a thumb at his own chest. "Me, I used to work for gun factories. I know boxed guns when I see 'em."

Doc Savage went to the customs office.

"The *Sea Mist* cleared for Cape Town, South Africa," they told him.

The bronze man kept his planes—he and his aids had several—in a Hudson River water-front boathouse hangar which resembled a down-at-the-heels warehouse. But the place had walls as thick as an old-time fortress and a bomb-proof roof.

Doc Savage took a plane and flew out over the Atlantic beyond Sandy Hook. He did not find a trace of the *Sea Mist*. Too much fog and darkness.

Near dawn Doc Savage joined Monk, Ham and the prisoner at the bedside of Johnny Littlejohn in Research Hospital. All but the prisoner seemed excited, the captive looking as if he were thinking about an unpromising future.

"Doc!" Johnny croaked. "It's astounding."

"It's remarkable!" Ham agreed.

Doc said, "You might try explaining what is remarkable."

Johnny was excited enough to try to sit up from the hospital bed in spite of his injuries. "It's a *Uer-Maa's*," Johnny popped his eyes excitedly. "Eighteenth Dynasty workmanship."

"You seem to be talking about a sacred scarab of ancient Egypt," Doc Savage said. "What is the connection with Harry Day, Doctor Collendar, and the missing Renny and Long Tom?"

Johnny said, "An absonous and daralogistic—"

"Whoa, dictionary!" Monk interrupted. "You get started with them words and nobody'll understand." The homely chemist looked at Doc Savage. "We searched the room of the safe-cracker. In a hole in the closet wall, we found this thing."

Monk unfolded a quantity of cotton batting and showed

an object about eight inches long and half as wide. It was a crusted mass of blue glaze, yellow gold, and scintillating jewels.

"Gimme back that!" the captive wailed.

"The pay he got for stealin' antitoxin," Monk explained.

Doc Savage scrutinized the scarab. It was, as far as he could determine, a genuine piece, as Johnny said; hence it possibly dated back to the Egyptian Eighteenth Dynasty, and thereafter degenerating until it suddenly disappeared at the end of the twenty-sixth Dynasty.

"They had more of them things!" the prisoner said plaintively.

Doc's flake gold eyes studied the man. "Who had?"

"Harry Day."

Monk rubbed the bristles on top of his head. "I'll say one thing for this mess: It's nice and mysterious. Man, am I confused!"

Chapter IX

SEA TRIAL

The *Sea Mist* vanished on the Atlantic like the *Flying Dutchman,* the spook ship of sailor legends. The United States Coast Guard did not sight her. Neither did the merchant ships of any nation. The fact that there was a thick fog for days helped explain this.

The missing men, Renny and Long Tom, did not appear in Doc Savage's skyscraper office, communicate with the bronze man, or show up in hospitals. Morgues did not report a body with big fists, or a body that looked as if it should have been on the slab years ago.

Doc Savage took a motorboat, a supersensitive electroscope, and Monk and Ham, and cruised the Hudson River, the Harlem River, Long Island Sound, and the seashore for fifty miles each direction from New York City.

Doc's assistants all wore shoes with unnoticeable inner soles of a metal which, while not radioactive enough to give them radio-poisoning, were active enough that the supersensitive electroscope would register at a considerable distance.

Thus the electroscope would indicate the presence of

any one of the men in a building, under the ground—or under the water. Doc hunted five days and did not find Renny or Long Tom with the electroscope.

He did not find any trace of Edwina Day. The pert little girl with the disposition of a Fourth of July sparkler had vanished as completely as had her brother, Doctor Collendar, and Snig Bogaccio.

"It seems everybody left on the *Sea Mist,*" Ham said.

For the next three weeks, Doc Savage was incessantly active. Net results of his efforts was a lot of police activity, a number of gray hairs in the heads of the bronze man's private organization of "graduates", and full-page advertisements in the newspapers offering large rewards for information as to the whereabouts or fate of the missing persons.

But there was no other result.

If it had not been for a young Swedish boatman, there might never have been any results. The Swede was sailing a tiny sloop across the Atlantic single-handed, and half-way across, he saw sun glinting from an object in the sea, put the tiller over and picked it up.

At first, he thought he had a plain blue clay jug, beautifully glazed. But closer inspection showed strange marks on the jug. The thing was corked, and the Swede picked out the cork. After he examined the jug's contents, he lost no time in flagging the first passing steamer.

Upon landing, the young seafarer turned up in Doc Savage's skyscraper headquarters in New York. He put the jug and its contents on the inlaid table in the bronze man's reception room.

"*Hvad betyder det?*" he said quizzically.

Monk came in and looked at the jug. "What's he brought? And what did he just say?"

"He picked the jug up in mid-Atlantic," Doc said. "And he's asking what it signifies."

Monk scrutinized the jug, scratched his bullet head, and said, "I've seen these kinds of marks before." He started for the laboratory with the jug. "Bet Johnny can translate 'em."

Doc Savage said, "The marks, as you call them, are ancient Egyptian hieroglyphics." Doc spread out a paper on the table. "This is more modern."

"Was that in the jug?"

"Yes."

Monk came over and leered at the paper. His mouth became a hole and his eyes almost got out of their sockets.

"Renny's writin'! *What's the date?*"

"Three weeks ago."

"Since they disappeared?"

"Yes."

Johnny, having come home from the hospital, was in a wheel chair, trying to convince Ham that modern principles of law had developed from the ancient Mayans. They stared at the paper when Monk presented it:

TELL DOC SAVAGE TO DIVE AT LATITUDE
18-47-3 s, LONGITUDE 29-11-16 w,
AND BE CAREFUL

                                          RENNY

The date on the message made it less than three weeks old.

"I'll be superamalgamated!" Johnny gulped.

"I don't savvy that!" Monk exploded.

Ham fumbled his sword cane and looked puzzled.

Doc Savage left them with the message and went back into the reception room to talk to the young sailor for a few minutes, and hear the young man refuse a reward. The Swede did, however, accept a note which would get him a job with a steamship line if ever he needed it.

"Doc," Monk said animatedly, "this latitude and longitude is a spot in the South Atlantic!"

The bronze man nodded. "Not far from the place where the diphtheria-ridden ship *Muddy Mary* sank, and where Doctor Collendar disappeared."

Ham dropped his sword cane, looked foolish and picked it up again.

"I hadn't noticed that!" he said.

Bony Johnny stared at the wall and groaned. It was a very pained groan.

"You feeling worse" Monk demanded anxiously.

"Worse mentally," Johnny grumbled. "I've got a hunch we've got to head for that spot in the South Atlantic. Here I'm all bunged up with broken bones and things." He doubled a fist and shook it as emphatically as he could with his one serviceable arm. "I'm going along anyway!"

He was wrong. They left him in New York, howling his head off.

Doc Savage put diving equipment aboard his yacht. That did not take long. Then they sailed, Monk and Ham bringing along their pets.

The yacht was slightly under two hundred feet in length, streamlined, and could make fifty knots at top speed, which meant there was not a craft in the world over speedboat size that could catch her. No craft of her speed could carry a gun of a size that would damage the yacht's armor plating, or a torpedo that would do much to her triple-walled hull.

The craft was known as Doc Savage's yacht, but that was a misnomer, a yacht being a vessel owned and operated for pleasure. This craft was a practical hooker, conceived, built and dedicated to experimental purposes. Her hull design had been copied by the U.S. Navy; she had broken through arctic ice after lost explorers, hauled refugees out of the Orient and gone to the South Seas for marine exploration.

The bronze man and his aids sailed from New York logging forty knots, which was cruising speed, and passed the *Queen Mary*, which had sailed hours before. Passengers leaned over the *Queen*'s rail with mouths open.

Doc Savage, Monk and Ham worked below decks. They could have used the assistance of the missing Renny's big hands. Renny was an engineer, and he had been factory supervisor when the diving bell they were going to use had been constructed after designs conceived by Doc Savage. Doc and his men were getting the diving bell in condition.

The yacht was crewed by graduates from Doc Savage's criminal-curing "college." They were highly trained, loyal, as efficient as men could be; and none remembered ever being a criminal.

The third day out, around midnight, Johnny called the yacht by radiotelephone from New York City. As soon as Johnny started talking to Doc Savage he used small words. For some reason, he rarely exercised his remarkable vocabulary on Doc.

"Doc," Johnny said, "another one of those jugs has been picked up with a note in it."

"What did the note say?"

"Exactly the same as the other one. This jug was picked up by a Portuguese tramp steamer which was on the lookout for it." The bony archeologist and geologist sounded puzzled. "It's mighty unusual for steamers to be picking up floating jugs."

Doc said, "I broadcast an offer of a thousand dollars for every note from Renny or Long Tom that was picked up."

"Then that explains it," Johnny remarked.

The next morning, the yacht plowed into a stiff northeaster, the sea first getting wind ridges that sailors call "varicose veins", then the tops began to blow off the waves, and after a while green seas were jumping over the bows and washing the length of the yacht. After that, any strolling on deck was done with one end of a rope tied around the stroller's waist and the other end fast to a davit or something else solid.

Monk stood on the bridge and suspected his complexion was changing to green.

Ham approached jauntily and said, "Dinner is coming up shortly."

Monk glared at him. "So is my lunch!"

Ham asked cheerfully, "Shall I ask them to serve your dinner here on the bridge?"

"Tell 'em to throw it overboard!" Monk snarled. "It'll save me the trouble!"

A bit later, Doc Savage found Monk seated on the bridge floor, holding weakly to a stanchion. Whatever Monk did, he did in a big way, including being seasick.

"Seasickness never killed anyone," Doc Savage said reassuringly.

"Ugh!" Monk croaked. "The hope I might die and have it over with is what's been keeping me alive!"

It was calmer the day following.

Johnny was on the radiotelephone again from New York.

Johnny said, "Doc, one of those jugs was picked up by a whaling ship, and another was found by an Italian cruiser. The notes they contained were identical with those in the other jugs, but they were signed by Long Tom."

"These notes were signed by Long Tom instead of Renny?"

Doc's great voice was a delighted crash that jumped the indicator needles on the radio transmitter.

"Signed by Long Tom," Johnny repeated.

"Then Long Tom and Renny are both alive!" Doc said.

It was rarely that the bronze man permitted himself the show of pleasure that he displayed now.

Johnny said cheerfully, "The fellows who found the jugs want their rewards."

"Pay them," Doc directed.

Monk braced himself against the radio room wall and looked as pleased as a green-faced man could.

"If they keep on findin' them jugs," he croaked, "it's gonna break us up."

Chapter X

WHERE LITTLE JUGS COME FROM

It was Sahara-hot in the middle of the Atlantic. The sea was a shining mirror that slowly bent and unbent. The sun blazed with enthusiasm, its brightness dancing gaily on winged fins of flying fish and sinking a dozen fathoms into sea water that was almost as clear as air.

The yacht stood still and rolled very slowly. It was taking a full minute to roll from its farthest lean to port to its farthest to starboard. The crew struggled with lines, donkey engines, shoring timbers and the big steel boom which was handling the diving "tank."

The diving tank was literally just that—a tank. At first glance, it could be mistaken for an army tank because of the big caterpillar treads. The walls were six-inch armor steel, windows almost a foot of the best pressure-resisting glass.

Collapsible arms on the exterior operated nets, or could clutch objects like hands and draw them into the tanks where they could be brought to the surface at the same pressure as in the depths. Batteries and electric motors furnished motive power and lights.

From a great swivel joint on top ran the cable by which the thing could be lowered into the sea. This cable now ran over a huge pulley on the end of a boom, like a fat bug and a stubby fishing pole. A roped catwalk extended out to the dancing diving tank.

Doc Savage, Monk and Ham walked out on the catwalk and got into the tank. The door was as ponderous as anything on a vault. They closed it. Doc picked up the telephone which operated through the cable.

"Lower away," he said.

There was vibration, and shimmering sea water covered the inspection ports. The depth needle crept around to fifty feet and Doc Savage said, "Hold it for tests."

The bronze man began testing the equipment which supplied oxygen.

Monk and Ham had never been down in a deep-sea diving bell, and they were not enthusiastic. This had led both of them to leave their pets on board the yacht. They tried to cover perturbation with a continuation of their eternal quarrel.

"Where'd you get that suit, you mythogenic?" Ham demanded.

Monk was one of the world's homeliest men, and his taste in clothing was almost as remarkable. For their descent, he had dressed in a frog-colored suit fashioned by a tailor with original ideas.

"I intend," Monk said with dignity, "to wear this suit out."

Ham peered through the thick ports at the water, which was still sun-shot at this shallow depth.

"For once," he said, "I wish you success."

Monk observed that Ham sounded a trifle worried, and he began to grin.

"If anything happens, we can swim to the surface," Monk remarked.

Ham winced. "Is that so?"

"I won't have any trouble swimming," Monk continued, "because I was a lifesaver once."

"Lemon-flavored, I'll bet," Ham declared.

Doc Savage completed his testing and said into the telephone, "Sink us."

There was a resumption of the vibration of the cable passing over the pulleys above. Water and an occasional fish passed the windows, and the light rapidly grew dim. When Doc switched on the electric floodlights, however, there was plenty of illumination outside.

There was no increase of pressure, because the interior of the diving bell was maintained at atmospheric level, regardless of the pressure outside. The only discomfort experienced by the inmates came from thinking about where they were. There was nothing physically unpleasant.

Monk settled himself for a long wait. The Atlantic was supposed to be a mile or so deep here, at least that was what the charts said. If they reached the bottom, they were lucky, Monk thought. Anyway, what could they expect to find?

According to the fellows called ichthyologists, who were supposed to know all about fishes, on the bottom of an ocean this deep there was nothing but strange-looking sea denizens: fish without eyes and fish which had eyes and were equipped with luminous parts like the common lightning bugs. Some of them carried their own lanterns, as it were.

It was Monk's idea of no place to be. Suddenly, the homely chemist thought of something. He shot to his feet so abruptly that he crashed his head on the low ceiling and fell back, dazed.

"I think there was a metal crash helmet on the yacht," Doc said. "You should have brought it along."

"Doc," Monk groaned, "I've just thought of something! Maybe the notes in the jugs were fakes! Maybe somebody dumped a few dozen of 'em in the ocean to be picked up."

"What would anybody do that for?" Ham demanded.

"So we would waste time diving after nothing!"

"By Jove!" Ham looked worried. "Why didn't we think of that?"

Doc Savage said, "If men's characters were as genuine as those notes, the world would be a much better place."

"If they were genuine, Doc, how would you tell?" Monk demanded.

"Monk," Doc said, "you have a secret mark, known only to you and myself, and it is understood you are to use this mark to prove anything you write to me is genuine."

"Sure. I haven't forgotten the mark."

"Neither had Renny and Long Tom," Doc said. "Their marks were on their messages, and proved—"

There was a bump of enough force that it upset Doc and his aids. They picked themselves up and peered out the windows.

Monk pulled his face back from a window and peered at Ham.

"Do you see what I see?" Monk demanded.

"If you see bottom, I do," Ham said.

"But there's no bottom for a thousand fathoms around here," Monk declared.

Ham looked at Doc. "How deep are we, Doc?"

"Not much over a hundred feet," Doc replied.

"See," Monk said to Ham, "we've only gone down a hundred feet. The ocean is a thousand fathoms deep. That's about six thousand feet, or more'n a mile."

Ham took another look through the window. He moved the rheostat controlling the floodlights and made them as bright as they would go.

"Well," he said, "we're setting smack-dab on something."

"Is it ocean bottom?"

"It's got the right color."

"Maybe," Monk offered, "it's the back of a whale we're sittin' on."

Ham frowned at Monk reprovingly. "It's no time for foolishness. The ocean is supposed to be a mile deep, but we hit bottom at one hundred feet."

"Personally, I think it's lucky we did," Monk remarked. "Because I don't think this thing we're in would sink a mile without something unpleasant happening."

Both Monk and Ham looked at Doc Savage.

Ham said, "Doc, did you know the ocean was only one hundred feet deep here?"

"I did," admitted the bronze man, "after I took soundings from the yacht."

The reply was unexpected news to Monk and Ham, but not surprising, for one could never be certain what would happen around the bronze man. That was one of the fascinations of working with Doc.

"If you knew it was only a hundred feet deep," Monk said, "why didn't we come down in ordinary diving suits? We could move around a lot better."

"There was no telling what we would find," Doc said.

"You mean—"

"I mean," Doc replied, "that this diving tank is the next best thing to a fortress."

Monk's spirits had risen briskly when he learned the bottom was only a hundred feet down. Now they took a dive.

"You expectin' some trouble down here?" he demanded anxiously.

Monk was afraid of nothing that walked on the earth or flew in the air, but he was not enthusiastic about anything under water. He could turn green at sight of a shark.

Doc Savage added, "Besides, there only seems to be a narrow ridge, with deep water on either side. We may have to look in the deep water for whatever Renny and Long Tom want us to investigate."

"My suggestion," Monk offered, "is that we mosey along the ridge first."

"That seems sensible," Doc agreed.

The bronze man picked up the telephone which communicated through the cable to the yacht above.

"Hello," he said.

In the next minute, he said "Hello!" five times.

"What's wrong?" Monk demanded nervously.

Doc Savage turned on a lamp which floodlighted straight upward. Then he peered through a ceiling window.

"The cable to the yacht seems to have been cut," the bronze man said.

Monk's large mouth came open and his small eyes got as round as marbles. He was thinking that the diving bell was too heavy to possibly be made to float to the surface. The way he understood it, they were sitting on top of an uncharted ridge in the Atlantic Ocean. His next thought was that they might slip off into really deep water.

"Whew!" Monk said.

Suddenly, he shot to his feet. He bumped his head again, but he was so excited he didn't feel it.

"*Cut!*" he squalled. "Doc, you said the cable was *cut!*"

Doc pointed through the ceiling window. "It was cut about forty feet above us. You can see the end."

Monk waved his arms the way he did when he was excited. "But it couldn't have been cut forty feet up. If any cutting was done, it had to be on the yacht, and that's a hundred feet up!"

"Look for yourself," Doc suggested.

Monk peered up through the glass. The cable end was like a shiny snake in the floodlight. And, as Doc had said, there was an end roughly forty feet long attached to the diving tank. The cable had been whacked off squarely.

Doc manipulated electric controls, and made a mechanical arm reach up, get the severed end and draw it close to the window for inspection.

"If you ask me," Monk blurted, "a cutting torch was used on that cable!"

"A good conclusion," Doc admitted, "judging from the melted appearance of the cable ends."

The diving tank was equipped with a radio for emergency use. The bronze man switched this on and spoke into the transmitter, then listened.

"The yacht reports the cable severed," Doc announced. "But they have noticed nothing unusual."

"The cut cable is unusual enough for the time being," Monk muttered.

"We're in no danger," Ham said.

"That's a matter of opinion," Monk replied dubiously.

Doc Savage turned a switch, and the interior of the diving tank began to sound like the inside of an electric company power house. Doc seated himself on a saddle on either side of which was an upright lever. The levers controlled the caterpillar treads which moved the tank. By slowing or stopping the tread on one side, the tank could be turned.

The tank swayed, jolted, and a cloud of sediment boiled up around the rear observation ports.

"We may run off the edge!" Monk said loudly. "We might drop off a cliff or somethin'!"

"Maybe not," Doc said, "if you keep a close watch for the edge of the ridge."

Monk glued his pug nose to the forward observation port. Instantly, his breath made steam on the glass, and he wiped this off. Then he let out a squall.

"Whoa! Whoa!" he howled. "Stop this thing!"

Doc halted the progress of the tank along the ocean floor and demanded, "What is wrong?"

Monk tried vainly to speak. He had to take hold of his own throat and shake it to get words loose.

"Look!" he croaked.

The cause of Monk's excitement was a crimson object about six feet high and roughly three feet wide. The thing seemed to be loosely made, for rippling motions went up and down it, and it swayed slightly. Monk was positive this effect was not lent by the water.

"One of the red mysteries!" Monk yelled.

Doc Savage grasped the light rheostat to put more illumination on the object. The rheostat was already over as far as it would go.

"We will move closer to the thing," he said.

"What's wrong with moving away from it?" Monk asked nervously.

Doc Savage ignored this advice, got on the saddle and shoved the caterpillar tread control levers forward. The tank moved about ten feet. Then there was a jerk and it stopped.

"We must've snagged somethin'," Monk muttered.

Doc made an inspection. Then his trilling sound became audible, and ranged up and down its strange scale with what struck Monk and Ham as more animation than it ordinarily held. Monk and Ham knew the trilling could only mean one thing: More trouble.

"Steel rods have been inserted in the tread wheels," Doc Savage said. "They are jammed."

Just from habit, Ham turned on Monk and said accusingly, "You inspected that part of the tank. Why didn't you take a wrench and try the nuts to see—"

Ham stopped with a gulp. He had just remembered there were no rods under the tank that could have come loose.

"Did you say rods?" he asked Doc.

"Yes."

"But there aren't any rods on the outside of the tank."

"That," Doc Savage admitted, "makes our stoppage peculiar, to say the least."

Monk bounded to the fore inspection port and peered.

"That red thing is gone!" he whooped.

At this, Ham looked as if he had swallowed an ice cube by mistake. "But I thought the thing was only a red seaweed of some kind."

"Well, it walked off," Monk told him. "Or swam. I don't know which."

Monk threw back the lid of a locker, dragged out a diving suit, and began drawing on the heavy rubber-and-fabric garment.

"Brothers," he said, "you can stay down here and have remarkable things happen to you. Me, I'm goin' up and see if the sun is still shinin'."

Ham said, "For a mythogenic, you don't have bad ideas."

Ham reached for another diving suit. These were equipped with self-contained oxygen apparatus, and the wearers could reach the surface without excessive discomfort—if nothing interfered.

"It might be safer to stay," Doc Savage said unexpectedly.

Monk and Ham peered at the bronze man. "What do you mean, Doc?"

For answer, Doc pointed at the ceiling inspection port. Monk's eye followed the bronze man's finger.

The port was obscured by something reddish in hue which rested directly against it.

"One of them is sittin' on top of us!" Ham gulped.

"As Johnny would say," Monk muttered, "I'll be superamalgamated!"

Doc Savage leaped to the controls which guided one of the mechanical grab-arms with which their underwater chamber was equipped. He brought the arm up, and opened it like a hand to seize the red object on top of the tank. He was not successful.

The scarlet object moved with unexpected speed, and they could observe that what appeared to be a wire noose had been looped over the grab-arm. This tightened.

Doc moved the grab-arm controls, and the motors groaned loudly, stopped, and overload circuit breakers made loud whacking noises as they opened. The line which had trapped the grab-arm was very strong.

"The other window!" Monk roared suddenly. "Hey! They're all over this thing!"

He could have saved his breath. The others did not need to be reminded that every window had suddenly been covered by a reddish object.

There was a series of thumps, grindings and hissings. Then the red objects disappeared from the windows, and it was intensely dark outside.

"They've put out the lights!" Ham barked.

Then Doc Savage flung with lightning speed to the entrance hatch and seized the T-shaped handles of the dogs with which the hatch was fastened. He began to pull inward on them with great force. The hatch was hinged to open outward.

In a moment or two, Monk and Ham comprehended that Doc was trying to keep the hatch from being opened from the outside. They sprang to his assistance. There was hardly room for all hands, but they did their best. They braced themselves and strained.

An inexorable force from without began to pull the hatch open in spite of all their efforts.

It came open enough to let a sheet of water in around the edges. The water pressure at this depth was so great that the incoming sheet of water was as stiff as a pane of glass.

When about half a barrel of water was inside, Doc and his aids got the hatch closed again. They got it closed rather too easily, Monk thought.

"Unless I'm mistaken, they stopped pullin' on the thing," the homely chemist muttered.

Ham looked at his arm. The arm was soaked by the sea water which had squirted in through the crack. Ham began to shake the arm and slap it with his other hand.

"Ouch!" he complained. "The infernal stuff stings!"

By that time, the others were beginning to realize the same thing. They had all been splattered more or less by the inrushing water, and as Ham had said, it was stinging.

That was about the last thing they remembered, for it suddenly became very black for all of them.

Very black—and very quiet.

Chapter XI

THE BLUE ZONE

Ham, Brigadier General Theodore Marley Brooks, was a Harvard Law School product, one of the best— the latter fact admitted even by Harvard. He had made a fortune practicing law; then, he had given way to his urge for excitement and adventure and had seized an opportunity to join Doc Savage in his unusual career of righting wrongs and punishing evildoers.

Ham Brooks was eccentric in three ways. First, he had an overpowering yen to go down in history as one of the best-dressed men of any age. Second, he had acquired his pet ape, named Chemistry because of the animal's likeness to Monk Mayfair, only to become extremely fond of the animal.

He ignored the ludicrous aspects of a dapper, highly educated gentleman of his caliber having such a pet. He did not consider it ludicrous, having become accustomed to Chemistry.

Ham's third peculiarity was his perpetual squabble with Monk. It was understandable that he and Monk should quarrel, for they were of opposite types, tastes and dispositions. About the only thing they had in common was the love of adventure which held them to Doc Savage.

They insulted each other liberally and at every opportunity. It had become classic with the people who knew them that Ham had never addressed a really civil word to Monk, and vice versa.

The real peculiarity about their quarrel was its falseness. It was a smoke screen. It was no more genuine, no more typical of their real feelings than the acted-out battles which appeared on the motion picture screen.

Monk and Ham were the best of friends, even though they went around threatening to feed each other to the first lion they found. But either one would risk his neck for the other. When they got in a jam, the first thought either man had was for the safety of the other.

So, when consciousness came to Ham, his first concern was for Monk.

"Monk!" he croaked.

"I'm all right," Monk's voice said. "How are you?"

"I'm all right," Ham replied.

Ham had not told the truth, literally. He was alive, which was something. But nothing else seemed quite right. Too, Ham missed his sword cane, without which he felt helpless.

Monk's voice had sounded small and queer, as though it had come some distance through solid rock. There was a definite bell-like quality about the voice. But it was undoubtedly Monk's voice.

Furthermore, Ham could see nothing but a luminous blue haze. He had decided this bluish fog was the result of a blow or something. It was generally believed that persons ordinarily saw stars when they were hit on the head, but some individuals saw a phenomenon like curtains of colored light passing before their eyes.

Ham was a colored-light experiencer, rather than a star observer. He thought he was seeing such colored lights now. He waited for them to go away.

In addition to the bluish glow before his eyes, there was a distinct odor in his nostrils. It took him a moment to identify it, then he remembered what it was. The odor was like the one noticeable by a person who has just had lightning strike very close. An ozone tang.

"Well, shyster," Monk's voice said, "when are you

goin' to quit starin' into space and look around at this funny place you're in?"

Ham suddenly realized there was nothing wrong with his vision, and that he had been staring straight upward. He rolled his head to the right, then to the left, and stared.

He began to wish he'd kept his eyes shut and postponed the thing.

Ham thought, at first, that he was surrounded by fog, and the fog was suffused with glow from powerful blue floodlights. The blue was about the same blue that is in the sky on clear days, but this color was not in the distance. It was close at hand. It was in the air!

When Ham held up his hand, the bluish tint was between his eyes and his hand, making his hand look blue, but when he brought the hand close to his eyes, he could see that the color was normal.

He had a sudden, terrible impression that he was no longer in air. *He was lying in blue gas!* He never knew how he came to leap to that conclusion so quickly, but he learned later that it was the correct one.

Monk lay on the left. Monk was tied hand and foot with stout-looking lines which, unless Ham was mistaken, were braided out of shark skin. Ham gave a flounce and perceived that he was secured in the same fashion.

Beyond Monk, and towering in size, was a surface of steel plates which, as nearly as Ham could judge through the bluish haze, were a reddish-orange, and black higher up.

Ham blinked at the great steel mass for a while before he recognized it as the hull of a steamship. They were, Ham decided, lying near the bow of the vessel.

Abruptly consumed with curiosity, Ham rolled away from the hull of the steamer and peered upward, seeking the name. When he saw the name, it gave him a shock he did not soon forget: MUDDY MARY.

"Monk!" Ham squalled. "You remember this steamer! She disappeared nearly a year ago. They thought she sank—"

Ham stopped shouting. He had turned his head and glimpsed the underside of the hull near the stern of the vessel. He could see very plainly that there was only half a steamship lying here. She was broken apart in the middle. *Only half a ship!*

Ham lowered his eyes with wild haste. He wanted to see if he was sitting on the bed of the ocean. He had an overpowering conviction that he was. The *Muddy Mary*, with a hole like that in her stern, must surely have sunk.

There was a thick coating of green growth underfoot, a mat of stuff which did not seem to grow upward, but was sprawled in all directions. Ham ogled the growth. He was not an expert on ocean growth, but he had seen this kind of stuff before.

They were sitting on a lawn of seaweed!

"Monk!" Ham yelled. "What—where—what—whew!"

"Yeah," Monk said. "My sentiments exactly!"

Ham's heart was pounding, and he believed this to be the result of excitement. However, the pounding was followed by a rush of giddy nausea and he lay back and gasped. He seemed to be surrounded by terrific pressure. The whole eerie blue universe around him seemed to be trying to cave in on him.

"I'm dying!" he croaked.

"Take it easy," Monk advised. "Doc said you might get that way if you exerted yourself. But Doc thinks we'll get used to it. Your system apparently accustoms itself, and you can move around."

"Where—is—Doc?" Ham asked with difficulty.

"He rolled back toward the stern of the steamer to see if he could find a sharp piece of iron and saw through the ropes around his wrists," Monk explained.

"Who—tied—us?"

"There you've got me," Monk said. "Doc didn't know, either. When we woke up, we were tied. That's all we know about it."

"Where—are—we?"

Monk looked uncomfortable and swallowed several times with some difficulty.

"I—uh—you want my opinion," he asked, "or do you want Doc's?"

"Doc's."

"He thinks we're on the bottom of the ocean," Monk explained. "But, of course, we can't be."

Ham didn't think so, either. He looked around slowly, gave their surroundings a thorough scrutiny, and there was only one other conclusion that presented itself.

"Monk," he groaned, "you know what I think?"

"I'm afraid," Monk replied gloomily, "that you think the same thing I do."

"I wasn't ready," Ham said.

"Neither was I," Monk confessed. "Do you reckon it'll be as tough to get in as they said it would be?"

"I hope not," Ham mumbled.

"Here, too." Monk frowned uneasily. "Do you suppose that guy will be at the gate to ask you questions, or do you reckon that was just an exaggeration that somebody put in during the course of history?"

"Saint Peter, you mean?"

"Uh-huh."

"I don't know," Ham said.

"He's supposed to have it all written down in his book," Monk reminded.

Monk suddenly grimaced and looked uneasy.

"What's the matter, Monk?" Ham asked.

"I hope he's got it down in the book the way we meant it, and not the way we said it," Monk said in a worried tone. "I've called you a lot of things, Ham, but I never meant half of it."

"I never meant half of what I said about you, either," Ham confessed.

The two paused to digest what they had been saying. The stillness around them came near being utter, and their physical conditions were decidedly uncomfortable. The force of a vise seemed to be pressing against them from all sides.

"So you only meant half of what you said about me?" Monk remarked thoughtfully.

"Why, about half," Ham admitted.

"I've been thinking of some of the things you've called me," Monk said. "Listen, you overdressed, ambulance-chasing excuse of a lawyer, if you meant half of what you said, I'm gonna roll over there and polish off your spirit or whatever's lyin' there talkin' to me!"

"Come ahead, you freak!" Ham shouted indignantly. "I never did like you! As a dead man, I like you even less than when you were alive!"

Monk endeavored to roll toward Ham.

"I'll run your spook ragged!" he promised.

At this juncture, Doc Savage put in an appearance.

The bronze man came walking from the spot where the front half of the steamer had broken off. His ankles and wrists were no longer tied, and he walked upright. However, he leaned far forward as he walked, and from time to time used his hands after the fashion of paddles. It was as though he were half walking, half swimming through the strange luminous blue atmosphere.

When he reached Monk and Ham and spoke, his voice seemed metallic and distant, as if it were penetrating a solid.

"How do you feel, Ham?" he inquired.

"I've felt better at times," Ham confessed. "What on earth happened to us in the diving tank?"

"They pried the door open enough to let water into the tank."

"I remember that, all right. About half a barrel of water came into the tank, then we got the door shut again. That was the last thing I knew until I woke up here."

Doc Savage said, "There was something in the water that stunned us."

"You mean," interrupted Monk, "the stuff in the water was like *chalam* juice?"

"What's *chalam* juice?" Ham wanted to know.

"It's a tree in Central America. The natives take the juice, throw it in the water, and it stupefies the fish so they can be picked up."

"In this case," Doc Savage said, "we were the fish."

The bronze man untied Monk and Ham. Monk picked up the braided rope which had secured his wrists and examined it.

"This looks like braided shark skin," he said.

"You are probably correct," Doc replied. "The inhabitants of such a place as this would naturally find it convenient to utilize many products from the sea."

Monk had reached the conclusion that they were not dead. This left only one possibility.

"Doc," he muttered, "are we under the sea?"

"It seems obvious that we are," Doc admitted.

Monk shook his head. "But that's impossible."

"Highly extraordinary," the bronze man corrected, "but not impossible."

"It's impossible as far as I'm concerned," Monk declared, and peered upward uneasily in hopes of seeing sunlight.

There was no sun. There was nothing but gaseous blue haze which was something like fog.

"We seem to be in some kind of gas that is heavier than water," Doc Savage said. "You can tell that when you move around. The gas doubtless lies on the bottom of a cuplike depression in the sea, and is covered by water."

Monk shook his head violently. "I've got a lot of respect for your opinions, Doc. But you're wrong. I can prove it."

"Prove it? How?"

"Because I'm breathing."

"Yes. One breathes from habit."

"But," Monk said triumphantly, "you breathe oxygen, nitrogen and some other stuff in a mixture. It keeps you alive. The weight of liquid oxygen is 1.132 grams per cubic centimeter, whereas water is approximately one gram per cubic centimeter, salt water being slightly heavier. Now, liquid oxygen might sink, but oxygen in gas form would be lighter than water and would float. Therefore—"

"You've gone far enough," Ham interrupted. "Everybody is suitably confused."

Monk waved his arms. He had some difficulty—it was as if he were trying to wave them under water.

"It's a scientific impossibility for breathable air to be kept under the sea, unless you confine it in a tank or something!" he shouted.

"They should have confined you in a tank at birth," Ham muttered, "and kept you there."

Monk made indignant poking gestures with his arms, and started to say more on the subject, but Doc Savage interrupted.

"Stop breathing," Doc said.

"Huh?" Monk looked puzzled.

"Stop breathing," Doc added, "and you will find you can get along down here perfectly well without it."

Half fearfully, Monk made a test of the suggestion. At the end of a minute or two, he looked utterly dumfounded.

"Great grief!" he squalled. "You don't have to breathe!"

Being perfectly human, Monk was frightened out of his wits for a few moments. His association with Doc Savage had brought him many strange excitements which he hadn't enjoyed at the time, but which he always looked back upon with delight, and which exerted a fascination that urged him to continue with Doc and get more thrills.

But Monk made a strong mental resolution never to go out of his way to get into another predicament like this.

"Whew!" he croaked.

The chemist in him began to arouse, and he took a strong scientific interest in their surroundings.

"The human body," he said, "can't get along without the oxygen and the other stuff that it gets out of the air."

"Which makes you conclude what?" Ham demanded.

"Well, you can't live without breathing!" Monk insisted.

"Well, you're alive, aren't you?"

"Yes, but—"

"There's no use arguing with a mentality like yours," Ham said disgustedly. "You're either dead, or you're alive. If you're alive, you're alive. Why argue about it?"

"Humph!" Monk said.

Doc Savage examined the ground and concluded that it had an upward slant to the left. He suggested that they head in that direction and ascertain whether there really was an ocean over their heads. Monk and Ham were very interested in making sure about that point, too, so they set out.

Chapter XII

DEATH IN BLUE

That is, they went through the motions of setting out.

Monk tried to start off with a leap, and it was a very successful leap, although slower than he had anticipated. He went upward several feet and hung suspended!

Monk was so astonished that his mouth made shapes for some words, and the sounds for different words came from his vocal cords. The effect was that of a dog fight.

Finally he got organized.

"Help!" he squeaked. "Gemme down! What's happened to me?"

He flailed both arms wildly, tried to reach for the ground, and as a result turned half a somersault and ended up with his back to the earth. And if anything, he seemed to go upward a few feet.

"I'm floating to the top!" he squalled. "Stop me!"

"Take it easy!" Doc Savage shouted.

Monk clubbed around madly. "Easy! I'm floatin' to the top, I tell you!"

Doc said sharply, "Stop waving your arms! You'll settle back down!"

Monk followed the suggestion. A few moments later, and he was back beside them.

"Whew!" Monk gulped. "You can *swim* in this gas!"

They set out again, holding themselves on the bottom by bending over and seizing handfuls of the rank growth. Monk was careful to try no more leaps.

The slope of the ground grew sharper. Doc and his aids found that it was very difficult to move; the effect was actually as if they were passing through a liquid even more difficult to displace than water.

There was a thick coating of rank plants and shrubs, some of these being quite large, taller than their heads. The branches and tendrils of these did not grow upward in the conventional manner. They had the apppearance of just growing in any convenient direction.

"You will notice," Doc Savage pointed out, "the evidence of a nonexistent sun. Plants on the surface of the earth, and even sea growth in shallow water, send branches toward the sun. There is no sun here, so the growth progresses in any convenient direction."

Monk seemed very much saddened by this comment. Ham peered at him curiously.

"Aren't you interested in scientific facts?" Ham demanded.

"I ain't enthusiastic about anything," Monk groaned, "that further proves we're in some queer gas pocket under the sea." The homely chemist looked plaintive. "How we gonna get outta here, brothers?"

"Just walk up to the water, and swim the rest of the way," Ham suggested.

"It won't work," Monk said pessimistically.

"What makes you think so?"

"Oh, it just sounds too simple." Monk addressed Doc Savage with a question: "Doc, can we walk to the water, then swim?"

"We might even swim upward in this gas to the water," Doc suggested.

Monk grimaced. "I'll walk, crawl, or whatever you call what we're doin'."

It had not slipped their minds that their main purpose was to find Renny and Long Tom. Also the two Days, Harry and Edwina, and Doctor Collendar and Snig

Bogaccio—if the latter individuals should be with Renny and Long Tom. Furthermore, nothing had happened to make it necessary to mention the matter. But they had not forgotten it.

Now Ham brought it up.

"Do you suppose Renny and Long Tom are down here somewhere?" he asked.

No one knew, so no one answered.

"I wonder," Ham continued, "What those red attackers were?"

"Look, shyster," Monk growled, "do me a favor and shut up."

"Shut up?"

"Say no more," Monk requested. "If we start wonderin', there's so much to wonder about down here that we're liable to all go bugs."

Ham showed vague signs of intending to resume his perpetual quarrel with Monk, but this activity was sidetracked when they encountered water.

"There it is!" Monk howled. "The ocean!"

Doc and his aids advanced a few yards more, then stopped to stare. The upside-down phenomenon confronting them—they were literally standing on a beach which sloped the wong way, at the shore of an ocean which was over their heads—was so unusual that they were held speechless for some time.

"All I can say," Monk muttered, "is that it's a blamed strange place for an ocean to be."

The juncture of the gas and the sea was a smooth one, and it was somewhat like standing in a bluish light and looking upward at the slick underside of a great block of greenish-black glass.

Whatever the nature of the glow which suffused the gas where they stood, it did not penetrate the sea water to any great depth, and since no sunlight reached to this point, it was rather like peering into a puddle of ink with a slightly greenish tinge.

"Climb on my shoulders," Monk suggested, "and you can reach high enough to stick a finger in and see how cold it is."

This remark drew a scowl from Ham.

Doc Savage put in quietly, "Now that we have confirmed the fact that we are under the ocean, it might be advisable to hunt for Renny and Long Tom."

Monk cocked one eye at the sea, sighed, and said, "Good idea. I ain't so hot about gettin' in that water as I was."

They held a consultation about logical ways of going about finding Renny and Long Tom. They concluded the only practical course was the obvious one: Just start out and hunt.

They consulted the wrist compass which Doc Savage wore—he was still wearing it, although their pockets and the bronze man's gadget-carrying vest had been rifled—and set a course due south. The route led downward.

Then they began to feel strangely tired.

Monk, having expended a good deal of energy, was first to feel the lethargy.

"Let's rest," he muttered. "I'm getting kinda logy."

Doc Savage and Ham were feeling the same way. Doc, in fact, was feeling much weaker than the other two. He was, he realized, not far from collapse, whereas Monk and Ham had strength enough to go a little farther.

Doc's condition was the exact reverse of ordinary. Scientific training and careful living had given him strength and endurance far beyond that of Monk and Ham. It was puzzling that he should collapse ahead of them.

"Monk! Ham!" he said abruptly. "Do not move. Don't waste energy. We are in a bad predicament."

The two aids stared at him. The bronze man never exaggerated, and if anything, he was given to the most remarkable understatements. In the past, Monk and Ham had seen him go through a thing where houses were blown up, ships sunk and dozens of enemies perished, then had heard Doc dismiss it as a "slight difficulty." If Doc said they were in a bad predicament, it was probably more than bad.

"Whew!" Monk croaked. "What is it, Doc?"

Doc said, "You remember your argument about whether we were getting the oxygen necessary for breathing out of this luminous blue gas?"

Monk swallowed. "Yeah."

"Apparently we are not getting it out of the gas," Doc Savage explained. "My fear is that we were made to swallow chemical pills while we were unconscious, and we have been absorbing oxygen, or some substitute, in that fashion."

"Blazes!" Monk exploded. "You mean that the pill is about dissolved and that makes me feel so weak?"

"I am afraid so."

"What'll happen when the pill is all gone?"

"Conceivably we may suffocate in this gas."

"You mean we'll die?" Monk yelled.

Doc did not answer. But the grim expression on his metallic features furnished Monk with an affirmative answer. Monk blanched and got to his feet.

"I'm gonna try to swim to the top before my pill runs out!" he yelled.

He started clawing over the carpet of seaweed, and soon collapsed. He started strangling and turning purple.

With considerable difficulty, Doc reached Monk's side. "We haven't enough strength left," the bronze man said. "Lie perfectly still.

With an effort that was obviously tremendous, Doc removed his shoes. He began to strike the heels together, and made a procession of clicks that sounded about like two rocks being tapped together under the water.

He tapped three times fast, tapped three times slow, then three times fast. He waited a moment, then repeated the combination of nine taps.

"As nearly as we can come to the code S O S," he explained.

Monk began to strangle and tear feebly at his chest. Ham was also down, and lying on his back, every muscle rigid with the effort of trying not to waste his energy.

Doc continued tapping the international distress signal.

Monk's purple color increased. His tongue came out. Ham gave way suddenly to his overpowering urge to strangle, and rolled wildly, clenching at his throat. Then he came to a stop and was still.

Doc Savage continued to beat out three short taps, three spaced ones, and three short ones. He was nearer the end than either Monk or Ham, but kept going ahead on sheer will power.

Chapter XIII

RED ANGELS

The red form was about six feet tall. There was an eerie flowing character about it, since the thing at first glance seemed to be propelling itself with two stubby wings, although walking on the bottom at the same time.

It resembled a queer red bird running along the earth as very large birds do when preparing to start flying. It stopped beside Doc Savage and squatted.

It was a man in a red coverall garment.

This was evident when arms were withdrawn from fin-like extensions on the red garment, and hands came into view. The hands held a small jar which contained dark-looking capsules.

The hands inserted one of the capsules in Doc Savages mouth, then kneaded his throat until he swallowed it. Monk and Ham were also given the capsules.

The man in the scarlet garment then settled down to wait. He produced a small disk-shaped gong and a hammer, both apparently of brass, and tapped the gong with the hammer. It gave forth a sharply penetrating note. About a minute later, the gong was tapped again.

The gong had been struck at least fifteen times before Doc Savage opened his eyes and got them focused.

Then several more red-clad figures emerged out of the luminous blue haze. It was plain that they had been guided to the spot by the gong.

They gathered around and stared at Doc Savage.

"Sono interamente annoyato di cio!" one of them said.

Doc Savage said, *"Grazie, signores."*

"Italiano!" one ejaculated.

"No," Doc Savage said. "Not Italian. American."

They shrugged as if it didn't matter.

"We did not know what nationality you were," the spokesman said in English which was nothing to brag about, but understandable. "We decided to try Italian."

"The one who had first spoken said, "As I said in Italian, we are vexed about this."

Doc replied, "And as I said, thank you, gentlemen, for saving our lives."

"You should have remained where we left you tied. By moving away, you were lost when the chemical necessary to your existence here was depleted. Had we not heard a sound you made, you might have met death."

"We had no way of knowing that," Doc said reasonably.

The bronze man had concluded that neither Italian nor English was the native language of these strange men. He knew he was right when they launched into a discussion in a tongue which at first struck him as being utterly strange.

Doc was startled. He could speak all the major languages of the world, and had a smattering of practically every known dialect. It was not conceit when he took it for granted that he could understand any language that would be spoken. He had put in a great deal of intense effort learning languages.

He could not comprehend a word these men said in their native tongue. But there was something vaguely familiar about it.

Monk awakened, listened to the cackle of voices, and rubbed his jaw in bewilderment.

"What kind of ducks are these?" he wanted to know.

The red-gowned men continued to talk. They had not exposed their faces, and all that could be seen was their eyes. These were visible behind slits in the scarlet garments. All the eyes were dark, with extremely large pupils. Hands were the only other parts of their anatomy which showed. The hands were the color of rich cream and had very long fingers.

They were growing more excited as they talked, judging from the increasing hand gestures. Doc Savage grew tired of the prolonged confabulation.

"We came here looking for Long Tom Roberts and Renny Renwick," Doc interposed.

"For who?" one of the red men asked.

Doc repeated the names.

"Will you describe them?" the other requested in his bad English.

Doc described Long Tom's appearance of a general physical wreck, and Renny's extraordinary fists.

"They are our friends, our comrades," Doc explained. "We came seeking them, and when we have found them, we will leave."

"We'll leave with the greatest of pleasure!" Monk interjected.

"We know of no such men as you describe," the spokesman of the red-gowned men said bluntly.

At once, the strange group resumed the discussion in their native tongue. Doc Savage listened intently, picking out words which were repeated frequently and cataloguing them with meanings akin to the words most often in the English language. He hoped that would give him a smattering of the lingo.

"What are they talkin', Doc?" Monk asked.

"Mystery to me," the bronze man admitted.

Then the palaver came to an abrupt end. The stares Doc and the other two received seemed ominous.

"This Renny Renwick and Long Tom Roberts," one red-robed man said, "are they with the one called Doctor Collendar?"

Monk gave a violent start. Without stopping to think, he yelled words.

"That's right!" he shouted. "Renny and Long Tom were—"

He did not finish because the red-clad men fell upon them as one individual. They had a great deal of muscular strength.

However, Monk was no milksop himself. In a space of seconds, he had one fellow's neck scissored between his knees, had two more by the throat, and was roaring the way he always roared in a fight.

"Monk!" Doc called loudly. "Do not fight them!"

"Fight 'em!" Monk howled. "I'll annihilate 'em! I'll turn 'em to grease spots!"

"Monk!" Doc said.

The bronze man's tone threw cold water on Monk's rage. The homely chemist subsided reluctantly, muttering, "But Doc—"

"Obviously they are enemies of Collendar," Doc explained. "That automatically makes them our friends."

Their assailants held them down, produced more cords of braided shark skin, and bound them tightly. Then they stood around in a silent, threatening ring.

"You are enemies of Doctor Collendar?" one asked sardonically.

"Exactly," Doc replied.

"You are lying, of course," the other said.

"But—"

"You are trying a trick as old as our race," the other said grimly. "You are trying to make us think you are friends, when you are enemies."

Monk, realizing his own words had precipitated their predicament, tried to straighten it out.

He said, "When I told you Renny and Long Tom were with Doctor Collendar, I meant they were prisoners. Collendar seized them in New York and brought them here. At least, we think he did."

The red figure made an unpleasant sound.

"When Doctor Collendar receives your legs in one bundle, and your arms in another, we will know the truth," he said. "If Collendar laughs, we will know you were his enemy."

"Now, listen—"

"Silence, you!" the other ordered.

"That's a fine attitude to take!" Monk complained.

The red-garmented man who had done most of the talking—Doc had gathered that his name was something that sounded like "Tukan"—spoke in a commanding tone. As a result of this order, the captives were seized, and a march through the strange blue domain started.

Two men grasped each prisoner by the arms, and traveled in a running walk, helping themselves along by flippering movements with their free hands which grasped a finlike arrangement inside the crimson cloaks. The captors were accustomed enough to traveling in the heavy blue vapor that they made surprising time.

They reached the half of the wrecked steamer *Muddy Mary*, and one of them produced a sound-making instrument something like a harmonica. It was larger than a harmonica, shorter, and the reeds were more powerful. The man blew upon this instrument. It had five distinct notes, and he blew combinations of these.

The trilling sound of the harmonica carried astonishingly through the gas.

Apparently the harmonica was a form of telegraphy, because men began arriving. They seemed to be scouting parties. After each one of them made a report, the man in charge seemed more dissatisfied.

"Somethin' queer is goin' on," Monk announced. "Don't they seem kinda worried to you, Doc?"

Doc admitted that they did seem bothered.

"They have nothing on me," Ham volunteered. "They have me worried, too. If you ask me, they meant that stuff about cutting off our arms and legs."

"That'll make Collendar laugh!" Monk growled. "But it'll be too late to do us any good."

Another scouting party arrived, and this seemed to be the last one. The members of this group were hauling several large fish along behind them. The fish were a conventional species found in this part of the Atlantic. Another march commenced.

There was one central column, dragging the prisoners and the fish. Scouts moved out ahead, at the side and the rear, at some distance.

"Kinda looks like they expect trouble," Monk hazarded.

The trouble, if any, did not develop.

The route of march led steadily downward, and the captives were aware of slowly increasing pressure. It was like being at a considerable depth in a conventional diving suit.

Doc Savage, by way of warning, spoke in ancient Mayan.

"In case any of us escape," he said, "there is one thing we must remember."

Ancient Mayan was a tongue spoken by very few people in the so-called civilized world, outside of Doc Savage and his companions. They had learned the language on a previous adventure, and used it to communicate when they did not wish to be understood.

"What do you mean?" Ham inquired.

"We are in the same position as divers at a great depth," Doc said. "If we try to reach the surface suddenly the reduction of pressure will bring on the bends. Be careful to come up slowly."

Monk said, "Nothin' would please me more than havin' a chance to get the bends."

The marchers came to a great cube of stone rearing out of the ocean bed. The blocks composing this, some of them a dozen feet or more in dimension, were fitted together so accurately that joints were almost unnoticeable. There was one door. It resembled a vault door.

The door opened, and the men marched through into a long corridor which had a stone bench on their side. The men sat down on the bench, and the door was closed. There was a wait.

Doc Savage decided the pressure was decreasing somewhat.

"We are in a pressure lock where pressure is slowly reduced," he volunteered.

After perhaps twenty minutes, they were hauled on through the corridor, down many steps, and out another door.

"Great blazes!" Monk ejaculated.

Doc Savage and his aids stood on a floor of alabaster white, under a ceiling of intense maroon. The atmosphere was still blue, so that the color combination was striking.

And more striking still was the first of the round balls, intensely black in color, which sat in the middle of the great floor. There were other balls beyond it, all jet-black, spreading out in neat rows, and growing in size in geometrical order.

"Like pyramided billiard balls!" Ham muttered.

"Yeah," Monk agreed. "And all the color of the eight ball that we're behind."

The density of the blue gas had been lessened by the air lock, and they were able to progress in a more normal fashion. Distances and sizes, however, were deceptive. They covered scores of yards, and began to realize that the first of the sepia balls, which they had taken to be small, was at least a score of feet in diameter.

They were all amazed, but Monk was the only one who voiced his astonishment.

"Boy, the balls in the middle must be *big!*" he exclaimed.

They marched among the strange black balls for some distance before it dawned on them that they were houses. This fact came out when one of the citizens was caught napping, and they were upon him before he noticed. He leaped inside and slammed the door, which fitted so well that its presence was hardly noticeable.

The fact that the fellow had showed himself seemed to enrage the leader of the group which had Doc and his two men prisoners. The fellow went forward, banged on the side of the black ball, then shouted. They did not need to understand him to know what he was yelling was heated and to the point.

A meek response came from within.

"Wonder why everybody's keepin' out of sight?" Monk pondered.

"Probably they were forewarned," Ham suggested gravely.

"Forewarned of what?" Monk demanded.

"Well," Ham said, "the shock of seeing you could have consequences."

Monk's neck grew red. "When I'm untied," he said, "my muscles will probably be pretty stiff."

"I hope so," Ham said cheerfully.

Monk glared ominously at the other. "I know what I'll do to limber up. I hope your bones don't break easily."

Monk had hardly completed this remark when they were dragged through a door into one of the larger balls near the center of the array of balls. They now took this array to be a city.

They were shoved through a door, and the door banged. They sprawled on the floor, still bound, and examined a room which had a low ceiling of stone, a stone floor, and four of the most solid and windowless-looking walls they had ever seen. There were no lights in the room, but the luminous quality of the gas made lights unnecessary.

A stone bench extended along one wall, and on this lay someone who was bound like themselves.

As one man, Doc and his two aids sat up to get a look at a fellow unfortunate.

The occupant of the bench was a small, pert, dark-haired person who inspected them without too much favor.

"Wouldn't my face be red," she said dryly, "if I had been depending on you rescuing me."

"Edwina Day!" Monk exploded.

Chapter XIV

THE ANCIENTS

Somewhat hollow eyes and lines of suffering around the mouth indicated Edwina Day had been through considerable since they had seen her in New York, but this did not keep their second inspection of the young woman from convincing them that she was a very pretty girl. Cute, as Monk had said, as a pickle seed.

Edwina Day seemed as surprised to see them as they were to observe her. Following the introductory remarks, there was mutual speechlessness for some moments.

"You might," Edwina Day suggested finally, "say something."

Monk rolled over to the bench, managed to sit up, and examined the young woman.

"I hope," Monk said, "that we will get along better than we did the first time we met."

"You'll go a long way toward establishing sociability," Edwina Day said, "if you can untie me."

Monk grinned. Edwina Day grinned. Ham rolled over to them quickly, sat up and grinned.

"Don't you want to get in on this tooth display?" the young woman asked Doc Savage.

Doc said, "Monk, if you will lie on your face, I'll try my teeth on the shark skin cord holding your wrists."

Doc worked above five minutes and got Monk free. Monk sprang up, and was about to untie the girl when Doc said, "Turn Ham and myself loose first, if you don't mind."

"I thought," Edwina Day remarked, "that Doc Savage was the soul of chivalry."

"Also the soul of caution, he hopes," Doc told her.

The young woman sighed.

"With the world what I've found it to be the last few days, I don't blame you," she said.

After they untied her, she sat up and let Monk knead her right wrist while Ham rubbed her left wrist.

"I'll attend to the ankles myself, thank you," she said hastily.

She must have been lying bound for some time, because she was so stiff she could hardly walk on her first attempt. With Monk and Ham furnishing enthusiastic assistance, she made several circles of the place, then made it alone. After that, she came over to Doc Savage, shook her head in bewilderment and made a request.

"Pinch me," she said.

"Eh?"

"If I'm dreaming this nightmare, wake me up," the girl ordered. "I've had enough of it."

"Won't do any good," Monk put in. "I tried pinching myself hours ago."

"You mean this is *real?*"

"I don't want to think so any more than you do," Monk replied. "But here we are."

"And what a place to be!" the girl sighed.

Doc Savage believed the girl's story would clear up a number of points. And he hoped it would verify some of the conclusions he had drawn.

They had tried questioning the girl in New York with no success. She did not take to being questioned. He decided to use a more subtle means of starting her talking.

"When your brother was enroute from Cape Town to New York on the *Muddy Mary*, a diphtheria epidemic broke out on the steamer," the bronze man said.

"Yes," the girl said, "that's right."

"The diphtheria epidemic caused a sailor to close the wrong valve and the boilers blew up and the *Muddy Mary* sank," Doc Savage continued. "By chance, it sank directly over this strange gas-filled pit, and settled on the floor of the pit. Your brother miraculously managed to remain alive."

Edwina Day said, "It wasn't such a miracle. Harry put on his deep-sea diving suit while the steamer was sinking."

"Why'd he do that?" Monk wanted to know.

The girl studied Monk.

"If a shark grabbed you and pulled you under the water, what would you do?" she asked.

"I'd hold my breath."

"Why? The shark probably wouldn't let go."

Doc Savage picked up the conversation again, saying, "The natives of this place took your brother and kept him. Then the diphtheria epidemic spread from the steamer *Muddy Mary* to the natives."

The girl looked at Doc Savage blankly.

Doc added, "Your brother suggested that they find a steamer, board it and get a doctor to fight the diphtheria. They did so. They got Doctor Collendar."

"Who told you all that?" Edwina Day demanded.

Doc said, "When they got Doctor Collendar down here, he told them they would have to go to New York and get a large supply of diphtheria serum."

Monk and Ham joined the girl in eying the bronze man. in astonishment.

"However, getting antitoxin was not Doctor Collendar's real reason for wanting to go to New York," Doc added. "His real objective was to get the help of a gangster leader named Snig Bogaccio. Doctor Collendar wanted Snig Bogaccio and the latter's gang to help him come back and get something from the place."

Doc Savage considered for a moment.

"Doctor Collendar, Harry Day and the red-clothed natives went to the surface of the sea, reached the African coast in lifeboats from the *Muddy Mary* which they floated, and sailed to New York in a suite of cabins which Doctor Collendar booked."

"Blazes!" Monk said. "Where'd you learn all—"

Doc said, "Doctor Collendar had enlisted some of the red men who went along to New York in his scheme to return here with the aid of Snig Bogaccio. The other red men and your brother were ignorant of the plot."

"Just after they left the steamer in New York, your brother learned of the plot. He and some of the red men had a fight with Doctor Collendar and his red men. The fight was in an alley.

"Later," Doc added, "there was another fight in Doctor Collendar's office. Doctor Collendar's faction won that one. Your brother and his red men had to go into hiding in that cottage near the seashore."

Ham said, "Doc, I don't understand how you know—"

The bronze man interrupted, "By that time, myself and my men had become curious about the mysterious fight with red men in an alley, and the presence of Doctor Collendar, a man who was supposed to have drowned, in New York. We went to question you. You called your brother to warn him, thinking I was Doctor Collendar.

"Doctor Collendar had your telephone tapped, and he got to the seashore cottage and seized your brother just as we arrived. They took him into the sea. They could exist under water by using the chemical pellets. It was very mysterious at the time."

Doc spoke swiftly, winding up his recital.

"Doctor Collendar then seized you, and my two men, Renny and Long Tom. Then he got the serum. He persuaded your brother to handle that part of the operations, even though your brother was a prisoner. They could not buy a large quantity of antitoxin without answering questions about it, so they stole it. Then you all came here."

The girl took a deep breath.

"Who told you all that?" she demanded.

"It was conjecture on my part," Doc admitted. "Based, of course, on what's happened."

"It's the swellest piece of conjecturing I ever heard," the girl said.

Monk clawed in his short hair with his thick fingers.

Monk managed to somehow always seem more ludicrous when he was astonished.

"You mean," he demanded, "that's what did happen?"

"Exactly!" Edwina Day declared. "Every nail was hit on the head as far as it went." She eyed Doc Savage. "Would you care for me to take the yarn a bit farther?"

"I was hoping you would," the bronze man admitted.

"I can't explain everything," the girl said. "But here goes: Your two friends, Renny and Long Tom, are still alive. They're alive because the red men wanted an engineer and an electrician down here who knew all the latest discoveries. They're nutty about science, these people are. And you'll find out they are no slouches at it themselves. They wouldn't let Collendar and Bogaccio kill Renny and Long Tom."

"That angle," Doc acknowledged, "was puzzling me."

"We got here," the girl said, "and Collendar and Bogaccio took over a small village. I understand it's where the fishermen live. They ran the fishermen out. Then they sent me on into this city to make a trade."

"Trade? What kind of trade?"

"Collendar wants to swap diphtheria antitoxin to them for what he wants. More than half these people are down with diphtheria. A lot have died."

"That may explain the fact that we saw no one around," Doc suggested.

"They're enforcing a form of quarantine," the girl replied.

"What," Doc asked, "are Collendar and Bogaccio after?"

"*Miyah baqq.*"

"What?"

"*Miyah baqq.* You know as much about it as I do. That's what they called it."

"Hundred bugs," Doc Savage said.

The girl looked puzzled. "What?"

"The two words mean 'hundred bugs' in Egyptian," the bronze man explained.

"Oh," the girl said. "Well, that doesn't explain much."

Monk said, "Egyptian?"

"They're Egyptians, all right," Edwina Day remarked. "But from away back, what I mean."

"How far back?"

"Oh, thousands of years, I gathered from what my brother told me." The girl frowned. "They were on a continent or something that sank under the sea. They must have been pretty scientific birds, even back in that day, because they built this place and made that luminous gas and everything."

Monk suddenly smacked a hand on a knee.

"I've got it!" he howled.

Ham demanded, "You've got what?"

"You remember that time we found a kind of vault under the sea with a lot of remarkable scientific things in it, and we decided it had been left by some prehistoric race that had reached a high development, then been wiped out?" Monk demanded.

"I wouldn't be likely to forget that!" Ham muttered.

"Well, I'll bet it was the ancestors of these people who fixed up that place!" Monk declared.

Doc put in, "Miss Day—how does it happen you are a prisoner here?"

The girl grimaced. "Collendar said these people wouldn't kill a woman. So he sent me with his offer to trade."

"And—"

"Well, he was wrong," Edwina Day shuddered. "They've promised to cut off my arms and legs and send them to Collendar to see if he laughs."

"That's got a kind of familiar ring," Monk grunted uneasily.

They devoted the next two hours to discussion. No information of any great consequence came out of this. The net result of considerable conversation was that they wound up by concluding the predicament was much worse than they had thought.

Monk, Ham and the girl agreed that they felt physically terrible, and worse spiritually. Even the black walls of the chamber in which they were confined contributed to a low feeling. There was something about the place that brought thoughts of a coffin.

"There ain't no windows!" Monk groaned. "We're liable to suffocate."

"If you suffocate," Ham reminded him, "it'll be for lack of pills. Have you forgotten there isn't any air in this place?"

"You think of the pleasantest things!" Monk complained.

Doc Savage questioned the girl about the chemical capsules. "How often do they administer them?" he asked.

"About every four hours, although Harry says the natives don't take the pills themselves because they've trained their bodies to absorb chemicals from the foods they eat."

The girl added, "I think my next capsule is about due, if that's what you were getting at."

Doc Savage examined the wall until he found the microscope crack which was the door.

"Replace the shark-skin cords," the bronze man directed. "Make them appear as nearly as they were as you can."

The girl looked doubtful. "I take it you plan to grab them when they come in. I hate to hang crepe, but it doesn't pay to monkey with these fellows too much."

"What do you mean?"

"They've got some pretty unusual weapons, according to what Harry told me."

Doc Savage said, "We'll have to take chances. We have to get away from them, rescue Renny and Long Tom, put Collendar and Bogaccio out of commission in some way, then do what we can for this diphtheria epidemic."

"All of which would be a small job," the girl said, "for an army."

About five minutes later, the door opened and a man in a red robe advanced into the room, while other scarlet-clad fellows waited at the door. The man approached Doc Savage, a capsule in his hand, and bent over to give it to the bronze man.

Doc reached up suddenly, got the man by the neck, and administered pressure to certain sensitive spinal nerve centers. The pressure temporarily paralyzed the man, and he fell.

Monk and Ham and the girl threw off their bonds and rushed for the group at the door. The blue gas here, while less dense than that outside, was still almost like water in the manner in which it impeded movement. So their progress across the room, a combination of swimming and sprinting, would have been ludicrous had it not been so serious.

Doc Savage did not join that part of the fight at once.

He paused long enough to grasp his victim's red garment near the hem, and shuck it off the wearer in the fashion that a mink is skinned. Then he yanked the garment on himself.

He was not surprised to find that the cloth was some kind of alloy metal mesh instead of fabric. After seeing Harry Day, in the beach cottage, fire bullets which had not taken effect, Doc had suspected something like that. Underneath the metallic mesh, there was a layer of very spongy material which was there for padding and perhaps other purposes.

He glanced at the door to see how Monk and Ham were making out.

Both men were sinking slowly to the floor. It was plain that they were quickly becoming unconscious.

Instead of going to aid them, Doc Savage seized the man he had just paralyzed, then retreated dragging the prisoner. Monk and Ham had obviously run into a chemical in the water and absorbed enough through the skin pores to stupefy them instantly. The same stuff which had knocked them out inside the diving tank.

Doc's victim was wearing long tights of the red metal fabric, and Doc hoped to strip these off and get into them. The cloak he had captured was a pullover with a transparent face piece behind the eye slits which he had not realized they possessed. Once the outer garment was belted tightly around the waist, forming a watertight juncture with the tights, they would form a protection against the stuff in the water.

He did not get the tights on in time.

Being made unconscious by the stuff in the water was no more unpleasant than going to sleep. As when you went to sleep, you were never quite sure when it happened.

The awakening was not much different. It happened suddenly. There was nothing, no feeling of unpleasantness, no consciousness of time elapsed, to show that a period of senselessness had just passed.

Doc Savage, who had spent a great deal of time in the laboratory trying to develop just such an anesthetic, lay for a moment and wondered how it was made. Then he discovered the red-robed man called Tukan looking down at him.

Tukan began speaking in English.

"Your attempt to escape was needless," he said.

"Futile, at any rate," Doc agreed.

"You see," Tukan said, "We listened closely to your conversation with the girl."

"You did?"

"And so we are convinced that you are not friendly with Collendar. We then held a discussion and reached a decision. We were coming to tell you of that decision when you and your two men made that attack."

Doc Savage sat up. They were still in the room, and were surrounded by red-robed men.

"What was this decision you reached?" the bronze man asked.

"Your lives will be spared," Tukan said, "if you can capture, or kill, Doctor Collendar and Snig Bogaccio."

Chapter XV

SUNKEN SHIP

Ham said for the seventh or eighth time, "Who do they think they are, anyway? Wanting us to fight their battles for them?"

Monk frowned at the lawyer. "What're you squawkin' about? We're better off than we were, aren't we?"

They had left the cavernous enclosure which contained the city of round balls, and were walking, if their form of progress could be called walking, through cultivated fields of plants. Some of the vegetation was familiar-looking, and some of it was entirely strange.

The people working in the fields wore blue robes instead of red. The blue garments were obviously for the purpose of covering only, and not fashioned of the chain mesh.

Doc Savage came from the rear of the marching column and joined Monk, Ham and Edwina Day.

"It is some distance to the spot where they left our diving bell," the bronze man explained.

They were banking on the radio equipment in the diving tank being undamaged by immersion in salt water at pressure. With it, they intended to communicate with Doc's yacht on the surface, and have materials sent down with which to cope with Doctor Collendar and his group.

Doc had been talking with Tukan and others as they marched. They were sufficiently impressed by the bronze man to converse with him as an equal.

Monk waved at the workers in the strange-looking fields through which they were progressing. "Funny kind of farmin'!"

The field workers were not cutting weeds or loosening the earth by cultivation. There were no weeds, and no sun or rainfall to harden the earth.

Each worker had a contraption like a hand cornplanter, or a greatly overgrown hypodermic needle. They walked along, jabbing these in the ground and pushing a lever.

"What're they doin'?" Monk wanted to know. "Looks like they're givin' their potatoes shots in the arm."

"Something like that," Doc admitted. "They are administering a chemical fertilized material to take the place of oxygen, nitrogen and other elements which the air does not contain."

They passed into an area where there was arching lattice work draped with what seemed to be green ropes to which were attached round objects the size of apples.

"Hey!" Monk said. "Them things look like grapes!" He stopped for a closer look. "Doc, they are grapes! But the vines ain't got no leaves!"

The phenomenon interested Doc Savage, and he mentioned it to Tukan. Later, he told Monk what he learned.

"They are highly developed grapes, all right," Doc said. "The size has been enlarged by scientific stimulus, and the leaves bred off the vines in order that all energy could go into the producing of the grapes."

"But vines can't grow without leaves!"

"The plant food is supplied in chemical form, making the usual function of leaves unnecessary."

Monk scratched his head. "These guys must be chemical wizards."

"They are," Doc told him. "In the use of chemicals, they are far ahead of the world outside. However, about electricity, they know almost nothing. That is why they were so anxious to keep Long Tom alive."

The diving tank had been moved from the spot where Doc Savage and his two men had lost consciousness inside it. Tukan and his men must have solved the means of locomotion. The big steel tank sat on the "beach." The sea was green-black above, in weird contrast to the azure luminance all about.

Doc examined the radio equipment.

"We will have to dry it out," he explained.

Inside a quarter of an hour, they had the radio in operation. The yacht should be only a matter of hundreds of yards from their position under the sea. In fact, they could hear her engine vibration at times, as though the craft might be cruising back and forth, searching for the diving bell with grappling hooks.

Doc tried a small amount of power in the radio transmitter, and discovered he had to increase it greatly. The bluish vapor was evidently semi-opaque to radio waves.

He raised the yacht.

"Good grief, what happened to you?" the yacht skipper yelled anxiously.

Not wishing to strain the credibility of his yacht captain, Doc Savage concluded not to describe the fantastic predicament in which they found themselves. While the skipper was well-trained, trusted Doc Savage implicitly, and knew the bronze man had a habit of becoming involved in remarkable situations, there was probably a limit to what he would believe. Doc left out all the details.

"In the main cabin," the bronze man said, "you will find about twenty steel equipment boxes. Put these in a cargo sling and weight them, so they will sink. Then use your radio direction-finder and locate the spot directly over this transmitter. After you have done that, lower the equipment boxes. They are waterproof, so you do not need to delay to seal them. In fact, haste is essential. Lose no more time than you have to."

The yacht skipper was evidently puffed out like a balloon with questions.

"Where are you?" he demanded.

"We are safe enough for the time being," Doc said.

"But what kind of spot is this?" the skipper yelled. "We've taken soundings, and the yacht seems to be over an old volcanic crater or something. The rim of the crater is less than a hundred feet below the surface."

"Please see to lowering the equipment," Doc requested.

"The officers are getting it together now," the other responded. *"A newspaper is radioing from New York City, demanding our position. They want to send a plane out to get photographs, and they want to know what we are doing."*

"Do not give out our position," Doc directed.

"What are we doing? I'd like to know myself."

"Conducting scientific research," Doc stated.

The yacht commander's agitation was understandable. Not only had he been worried sick over the mysterious parting of the diving tank cable—Doc had learned from Tukan that the cable had been burned in two with a chemical preparation—but the yacht captain also had no idea of the real reason for Doc's wild rush to this part of the Atlantic.

The bronze man's behavior had seemed senseless. The captain knew it wasn't, but he also would have liked to know the reason.

Doc's neglect to inform the man of what was really going on was in keeping with a usual policy. The fewer who knew of the bronze man's plans, the less chance of a leak. Not that his associates would talk willingly. But there are forms of torture that will make any man talk, and truth serums which are also effective.

The yacht captain said, *"Our under-sea listening devices have been picking up queer sounds. There was a kind of musical note, something like a harmonica."*

He had heard the signaling device which Tukan's men used.

"Do not worry about it," Doc Savage suggested.

"We sent divers down to look for you," the skipper announced.

Tukan was suddenly at Doc Savage's side. "Ask them what they found!" he ordered grimly.

Doc relayed the inquiry.

"Well, the divers went down to the ridge," the man on the yacht responded. *"And they found what seemed to be a pocket full of what they decided was a gas with a blue color. They were uneasy about venturing into the stuff, and came back up."*

Tukan was beside Doc, scowling.

"Tell them not to come down again!" he snarled. "No one must ever know of the existence of this place!"

Doc Savage did not change expression.

"We are investigating the blue gas now," he said. "You need not bother to send more divers down. Merely lower our equipment."

Monk was not as calm. The homely chemist was struck with the last part of Tukan's statement, "*No one must ever know of the existence of this place!*" That did not sound so good.

When the yacht captain was fully silenced, if not satisfied, and Doc Savage moved aside, Monk went over and whispered to the bronze man.

"You hear that crack Tukan made?"

Doc nodded.

"Don't look like they're figurin' on lettin' us go, even if we do get Collendar," Monk suggested.

"The agreement," Doc said, "was that they were to spare our lives if we disposed of Collendar and Bogaccio.'

"But—"

"One thing at a time," Doc said. "We'll attempt an escape from this place in good time."

The radio was still switched on.

Suddenly, there was a terrific concussion. It came partially from the radio, but more from the sea. It was as if they were under a ceiling, and the ceiling had been struck a terrific blow. Their eardrums seemed to rip wide.

Instinct sent their eyes upward. What they saw was fantastic. The sea came surging down as though driven by a great hand, boiling, flying into strange foam in the blue gas. This down-driven brine spread apart, and began to rise again.

Monk shouted. Then he looked foolish, and grabbed his ears. He could hardly hear himself. He sank to his knees, for his chest, his whole body in fact, felt as though it had been crushed. Tukan and the red men were staggering about, dazed.

Doc Savage stumbled to the radio. The instrument, protected in its watertight case, still functioned. Seizing the microphone, he began to call the yacht in loud, anxious persistence.

"Explosion!" yelled an excited voice from the boat. *"Under the hull! Must have been a floating mine or something!"*

Doc Savage turned quickly, made for the dazed Tukan with a violent diving motion, and got the leader of the strange red men by the throat.

Tukan shook his head frantically.

"Collendar!" his lips formed.

Doc thought so, too. He released Tukan, returned to the radio and spoke rapidly.

"Abandon ship!" he ordered.

"Most of the men were already off!" yelled the yacht voice. *"The boat is going down fast."*

"Anyone killed?"

"No. Engines were shut down, so no one was below. Some are hurt, but not seriously, I think."

Doc said, "When you are in the lifeboats, get away from this spot!"

"But we've got to pick you up!"

"Get away from the vicinity!" Doc ordered. "Move at least fifteen miles away and stand by. We'll call you by radio when we need you."

"Right," said the man on the yacht. *"Here comes the water! I've gotta beat it!"*

Shortly thereafter, the other radio transmitter went dead.

Doc Savage stood by the underwater radio, turning it to the frequency of the small sets in the lifeboats. All the lifeboats were radio-equipped. Also, they were of unsinkable construction, Diesel-powered, fitted with shelter cabins, and well supplied with food.

In addition to the motors, they were center-rigged with sail. In an emergency, they were perfectly capable of crossing the Atlantic unaided. The yacht crew would be safe enough. Providing, of course, Collendar and Bogaccio did not get to them.

Ham said suddenly, "I wonder what became of the steamer, *Sea Mist,* that brought Collendar and Bogaccio?"

Doc had been pondering the same question.

"Probably standing by just over the horizon somewhere," he decided.

They were listening intently for any sounds the sinking yacht might make when it struck bottom—and instinctively wondering what the sounds would be like.

The noise was something like an egg being crushed slowly in the hand. It came from the right.

"Outside the gas!" Doc said. He was disappointed.

Since the blast which had ripped the bottom from the yacht, Monk had been seated on the ground, industriously feeling parts of his anatomy, and seeming disappointed when he found himself intact.

"Dang all oceans!" he complained. "Double dang 'em, in fact!"

Ever since they had first entered the diving tank, Monk had been gloomy. He was usually the most cheerful of Doc's crowd when they were in trouble. The change in the homely chemist was unusual enough to worry Ham.

"You're hurt?" Ham demanded.

"You bet I'm hurt!" Monk snarled. "All over!"

Ham said, "You're not hurt any more than the rest of us. Don't you think we get tired of your beefing?"

Monk snorted. His snort, in the dense gas, was a sound about like a piece of paper being torn.

"I sure know what a dynamited fish feels like!" he grumbled. Suddenly, a new fright seized him. He leaped and grabbed Doc Savage. "Habeas Corpus! My pig! He was on that yacht! Is he all right?"

Ham also jumped forward. "And what about Chemistry?" he shouted.

A few minutes later, Doc Savage got in touch with the radio-equipped lifeboats, learned the pig and the runt ape were safe with the yacht crew, and Ham looked more cheerful. Monk kept his long face.

Doc said, "The equipment we wanted is still on the yacht. We can try to get it."

Tukan and his red-clothed men signified their intention of going along. They did not, it was plain, entirely trust Doc Savage and his two men.

Chapter XVI

SEA TRAP

The operation of leaving the blue gas and penetrating the sea was a weird one. The sea was black and utterly ominous, cold on their skins as well. Cold enough that for the first time they realized the temperature of the blue gas must be somewhat near that in a well-heated greenhouse.

It was difficult also to adjust their minds to the fact that they could walk into the water and live without wearing diving suits or bulky paraphernalia for purifying their breath and supplying oxygen. The chemical capsules took care of that. All they had to do was to be sure and not breathe in the sea water.

To stop breathing, they discovered, was a physical feat. The first minute or so was not so bad, but after that, there was an overpowering urge to resume respiration. The unconscious breathing habit of years was not easily denied.

Monk failed completely on his first attempt, got his lungs full of stinging salt water, and had to be dragged back into the gas and emptied out. When he finished hacking and gagging, he had a great deal to say about the blue world under the sea, none of it complimentary.

"If I ever get outta this," he promised, "I'm even gonna quit takin' baths!"

They mastered the art of not breathing—Tukan and his men were practiced enough that the trick did not bother them at all—and worked into the sea slowly. They made, as nearly as they could judge, for the spot where the sinking yacht had landed.

The intense darkness of the sea was not the handicap they expected. Tukan and his men produced metal cases from which they drew transparent containers of glass or some similar substance. Inside these was a phosphorescent chemical which gave forth a brilliant blue light that penetrated the sea for some yards.

Monk, forgetting himself, all but opened his mouth and tried to talk. He remembered in time and used his fingers. Doc and his men were experts at the finger talk used by the deaf and dumb.

"Reminds me of lightnin' bugs!" Monk formed on his fingers.

It was Doc Savage, moving well ahead of the others, who heard a slight sound in the water. He stopped, signalled the others to halt also, and listened.

The sound did not come again. But the bronze man was suspicious. He decided to send the others back and go ahead to investigate.

Directing the others back developed into a problem. Doc could convey his wishes to Monk and Ham with ease, but Tukan and his men didn't understand the sign language, and had no wish to go back anyway. They ignored every gesture.

Monk and Ham then tried to head them back, with no success. Doc tried writing out a command on the sandy ocean floor. Tukan and his followers looked at it, then shook their heads.

Finally, Tukan understood that the bronze man suspected danger ahead. Results were not as expected. Tukan motioned for Doc, Monk and Ham to bring up the rear while he and his men led the way.

They led the party straight into an ambush.

There was a whirring sound. It was a small sound at its source, but since water transmits sound well, it was distinct. It grew louder and became a whine. A comet appeared with a steel nose and a spreading tail of bubbles.

A small torpedo! Doc Savage recognized it instantly. He lunged backward, jabbed his men, pointed at the torpedo. They understood, wheeled and dived wildly to one side. Remembering the effects of the previous blast on their ears, they protected these members with palms.

The torpedo was timed. Somewhat poorly timed, fortunately. It loosened flame and impact some distance ahead of Tukan and his men. But even then, effects, were dismal. The others, stunned and helpless, were tumbled backward by the effects of the blast. Like red sacks carried in a tide.

Doc Savage and his two men, expecting the blast, were ready for it. They were also farther away. They were tumbled some distance by the water rush, and got about the same impact as if they had fallen off a six-foot wall and landed flat on their faces, but there were no disastrous results.

They regained balance.

"Go back," Doc ordered on his fingers.

Monk and Ham nodded, turned and set a course for the domain of blue gas. Monk had a compass on his person, so they were not likely to get lost.

Doc Savage swam sidewise and upward. Ordinarily, with air in the lungs, the human body has buoyancy in water. But the bronze man's lungs now contained the luminous blue gas which was heavier than sea water, and the added weight was enough to keep him on the bottom. It was possible to swim upward, just as man with lungs air-charged can swim downward.

There was another explosion. Distance made this one less agonizing. Doc continued to swim. His objective was the wrecked yacht, and he hoped to reach it over the heads of the assailants, who undoubtedly were Collendar's men.

The intense blue chemical flares had gone out. Either the torpedo blasts had shattered the containers, or Tukan's men had extinguished them.

Frequently, as he swam, the bronze man tasted the sea water. And suddenly he tasted oil so strongly that it was almost nauseating. He knew then that he was over the yacht's ruptured fuel tanks, which were still emptying.

He swam down.

The yacht lay on her side. Doc came down almost upon the great bite which the mine had taken out of the hull. He clung to the jagged metal for a time, listening. There was no sound to indicate Collendar and Bogaccio and their men were close.

He swam along the deck to the boom by which the metal net sling would be attached. He had ordered his equipment cases lowered; it was his hope that they would still be in the net.

They were—stout metal cases, waterproof and shockproof. Almost twenty of them, hence far too many for him to take away unaided. He explored among them, selecting.

The equipment cases were numbered, and the numbers were raised so they could be read in the dark—or under the water.

Doc took five cases, and with a small line which had been used to lace the net shut, he strung the cases together, one behind the other. He jumped overboard with them, and towed them away. The towing was labor.

He dragged the boxes directly south. They made a plain trail, but the bronze man kept towing them until he reached a spot where the bottom was rock. Then he gathered the boxes together, bound them into a tremendous pack, and carried them, balancing carefully. He changed his course now, and headed directly toward the zone of blue gas.

When Doc slid down out of the sea into the blue zone, it was almost as welcome as coming out of the water into sunlight. He was tired.

Red-clad figures approached him almost at once.

Dropping the cases, the bronze man opened one quickly, and got out one of the electrical harpoons which they had perfected for underwater defense against sharks. The thing functioned off a high-voltage battery, and the current from this was stepped up and interrupted until it would deliver a stupefying shock.

The red-cloaked figures spread out in a fan. Doc joined together the sections of the shocking spear, set himself for defense.

He lowered the spear and made his widest smile when he saw that the ominous group was led by Tukan.

Tukan seemed puzzled. Angry, also. Then his anger gave way to doubt, and at last, understanding.

"It was our belief that you led us into a trap at your yacht," he said in his queer English.

"We were all led into a trap," Doc admitted. "Collendar and Bogaccio must have been tuned in on my radio conversation with the lifeboats. Knowing the equipment was about to be lowered, they would guess we would go after it."

"Can others listen to your radio?" Tukan asked.

"Of course."

"I and my people know nothing of radio," Tukan explained. "Is it part of this thing you call electricity?"

The incongruity of a people with such chemical knowledge, and such ignorance of electricity, struck Doc once again as they started the march toward the cavern wherein lay the city of houses that were like round black balls.

Chapter XVII

THE HUNDRED BUGS

Monk, Andrew Blodgett Mayfair, sat on a low stone bench in front of another and higher bench on which were jars and bowls probably containing food. Monk was ordinarily a hearty eater, but evidently the meals served here did not appeal to his taste. He was entertaining himself.

Monk's self-entertainment consisted of drawing a deep breath, holding it, then blowing it out as quickly as he could. Because the luminous gas was compressed in his lungs, there was a definite and almost flamelike flare each time he blew it out violently.

"Something wrong with you now?" Doc Savage asked.

"Everything," Monk said generally.

He pulled in another breath, held it and blew out a fiery guest.

"He's practicing up to be a dragon," Ham explained.

"For you," Monk told the dapper lawyer, "the fruit of the razzberry bush." The homely chemist looked forlorn. "Can I help it if there ain't anything to do but blow fire? They caught me and Ham when we came tearing out of the ocean. They must've figured we had killed everybody else or somethin', because they grabbed us and brought us to this billiard ball pocket."

"They were no more gentle about it than the law allowed," Ham added.

Monk pointed at the food disgustedly.

"What do you think they eat down here?" he yelled.

"Chemicals," Doc said.

"Chem—aw, you knew about it!" Monk scowled. "I'll bet Ham knew about it when he persuaded me to order up this dinner."

Ham smiled pleasantly. "I consumed my share of the food, and it was not bad."

Doc Savage directed the red men who accompanied him to array the equipment cases on a stone bench.

Meantime, Monk dipped a shovel-shaped eating implement into one of the containers before him. He let a bummy-looking mess drip back, and registered disgust.

"Proteins, I'll bet a dollar!" he grumbled. He dipped into another bowl. "And this looks like carbohydrates."

Doc Savage began to take articles from one of the equipment cases. Monk and Ham stared at the items he was removing. It was a large standard kit of medicines and equipment, the type of kit carried by country doctors who never know what they'll be called on to treat next.

"You going to tackle this diphtheria epidemic, Doc?" Ham asked.

The bronze man admitted such an intention.

"But can you do much without antitoxin?" Ham demanded.

"We'll see." The bronze man picked up the medicine bag. "Want to come along? You have both been vaccinated against the stuff."

The black balls which were the houses were not, as they had first thought, constructed of stone. They were fashioned, instead, of a composition not unlike bakelite.

Doc inquired about this. The black material, as he had suspected, was a by-product in the numerous chemical activities which were carried on.

"Why the ball shape to the houses?" Monk demanded. "It don't look practical to me."

The globular architecture, it developed, sprang from a simple and primitive reason. In some respects, these strange people were still utterly primitive. Their religious beliefs, for instance, were quite profound. Theirs was no go-to-church-on-Sunday-and-raise-hell-the-rest-of-the-week religion. It was a religion that filled their lives and colored almost everything they did.

Tukan's answer, when asked why the houses were round, was an example.

"Only an infidel and one of evil ways would live in a house which was not round," he said.

Doc asked a few more questions, and learned that the ancestors of these people had been sun-worshippers, and had lived in ball-shaped houses because the sun was round. Down to their descendants had come the quaint idea that to live in a house that was not round, was one way of going to hell.

The great ball in the center was the temple of Tukan, who was high priest. When they asked to view the interior, he at first hesitated, then agreed.

"My reason for taking you," he said pointedly, "is not to satisfy your curiosity."

"And what is your reason?"

"In the temple," said Tukan, "is the cause of all this trouble."

"*Miyah baqq?*" Doc Savage asked.

Tukan looked at them strangely, then remembered and nodded. "Yes. The young lady told you of *Miyah baqq*. And that reminds me!"

He clapped his hands, said something in the native tongue which Doc Savage could not understand. Two red-clothed men departed. When they rejoined the group, they brought small, pretty Edwina Day.

The girl looked relieved.

"Whew!" she said. "I thought they were leading me out to the block, or wherever it is they use to take off the arms and legs."

Ham said politely, "You needn't worry about that. I fixed that up for you."

"*You* did?" Monk looked indigant. "You didn't have any more to do with it than I did, and I didn't have anything. It was Doc."

Ham smiled at the young woman. "I hope you won't let Monk alarm you. He has a wife and seventeen poor unfortunate children who all look like their father. Sometimes it preys on his mind until he's not himself."

Monk, who had never had a wife, let out a howl.

"That's a lie!" he squalled. "That's—that's—" He couldn't think what it was, and sputtered.

Doc Savage steered Tukan away from the quarrel, and put questions under the guise of conversation. He was curious about the language. He learned that it was an offshoot of the Egyptian tongue spoken during the Eighteenth Dynasty and earlier.

That accounted for the familiar quality in the tongue, for Doc was familiar with ancient Egyptian languages, although naturally he had never heard them spoken. For that matter, there was a scattering of modern Egyptian in the language.

Miyah baqq was an example of carry-over of words. The modern Egyptian words *Miyah baqq* translated generally to mean, "hundred bugs." Doc gathered that this translation would apply to the *Miyah baqq* here in this strange lost place.

He was shunted off the subject before he could learn any more on the point.

"Have you no curiosity," Tukan asked, "about how we came to know your language, English? And I recall that we spoke to you in Italian at first."

Doc Savage was not as curious about that as he was about the "hundred bugs." There could be only one explanation of how these people could speak modern languages. However, Tukan showed definite intentions of sidetracking the subject of *Miyah baqq*.

"You could have learned English from Harry Day," Doc Savage said.

"We spoke English long before Harry Day came," Tukan said proudly. "And Harry Day did not speak Italian."

"Of course," Doc said, "Harry Day was not the first man who came here from the outside world."

Tukan smiled. It was the first time Doc had seen him show any emotion other than flashes of rage. He was a serious-minded fellow.

"When the sea has cooled one hundred times," Tukan

said in his queer-sounding English, "we send forth an expedition of our strongest high priests. They travel upon the sea until they find a ship. They seize the ship and bring it to this spot, and the sailors are brought down to become like our people."

"Isn't that a little hard on the sailors?" Doc asked dryly.

"We must have knowledge of the outer world," Tukan said, as if that explained everything.

In speaking of coolings of the sea as a measurement of time, Tukan unwittingly referred to years. The sea, of course, would grow slightly cooler with the advent of the winter seasons. One hundred coolings would mean a hundred years. Their method of getting information from the outside world was rough and cruel, but at least they indulged in it infrequently enough.

"We got our last ship nearly ninety coolings ago," Tukan sighed at the memory. "It was before my day. I have lived through only sixty coolings."

Doc glanced at the man sharply, and his estimate of the life here took a sharp rise. The high priest was sixty years old, was he? Forty would have been a long estimate.

Tukan sighed again. "The last ship was a monster. It's length was from there"—he pointed—"to there."

Doc judged the length at slightly over a hundred feet.

Tukan nodded solemnly. "And it had upon it strange iron pipes of great diameter, called cannons. They burned a mixture of saltpeter and other ingredients, and coughed an iron ball a great distance in the outside world." He smiled. "Down here, they only made a great jar, and the iron ball was scarcely coughed out of their mouths."

Doc had already decided that firing a cannon down here would not be greatly different from firing one under water. If it didn't blow up, the cannon ball would be stopped abruptly by the heavy gas.

Tukan heaved another sigh. The deepest one of all.

"My priests who went with Harry Day tell of ships of incredible size and speed, and they tell of man-made chariots in the sky which travel with the speed of sound." The high priest frowned. "It may be that they lie. This Collendar is a devil. I sent my most trusted priests with him, and he managed to turn fully half of them against us."

"How did he turn them against you?" Doc asked sharply.

"By making them believe that they would all be high priests in your world," Tukan explained. "He told them that they would have much money, and that men used money to buy power over other men in your world."

Ham, having lost his argument with Monk, came up in time to hear that last.

"Collendar was about right, at that," the lawyer remarked.

Tukan said, "We will enter the temple."

They stood looking up at the great black temple ball. It rounded up, it seemed, to infinity. Alongside a New York skyscraper, it would have been remarkable for its unique shape rather than its size, probably.

But here in this luminous blue haze where an object a hundred feet away was as dim as though it had been a mile distant, the proportions of the temple ball were awesome.

They entered through a portal guarded by four priests in red garments. Beyond was a line of red-robed priests to the right, and red-frocked priestesses to the left.

Monk gave the priestesses a long, eye-popping stare.

"Brothers," he said, "I've been underestimating this place!"

The feminine contingent of the priesthood obviously did not go in for the full-draped dress habits affected by the priests. The contrary, rather.

Their skirts were red brevities, and covering elsewhere was at a minimum. They wore, however, enough jeweled ornamentation to make up for any other garment shortcomings. Their headdresses were elaborate, their anklets numerous and heavy and studded with brilliants.

Even their fingers were heavy with rings, and each young lady—they seemed to be uniformly young—wore on her left wrist a ring-and-bracelet-connected-with-a-scabbard arrangement which held a small dagger.

Monk ambled over for a closer look.

"Not bad," he said frankly. "For years, I've been hoping Santa Claus would bring me something like one of these."

Tukan, frowning, said, "They are the High Priestesses. They do not marry."

"Who said anything about marrying?" Monk wanted to know.

Ham, who had moved over to the side of Edwina Day, suddenly deserted that young woman and went over to inspect some of the High Priestesses.

Edwina Day said, "My magnetism must be slipping!"

"I'm looking at these gaudies they're wearing," Ham explained. He sounded awed. *"They're real!"*

"Real what?" Edwina Day asked.

"Real gold and jewels." Ham swallowed several times. "There's enough right here on these girls—priestesses, I mean—to sink a navy."

"And build one, too," Edwina Day remarked.

Tukan said impatiently, "We have much to do! Let me show you the *Miyah baqq*. And we will leave."

He led the way down a long corridor, up many steps, and stopped, pointing.

"There," he said.

They were hideous. They were the only utterly ugly things Doc Savage and his men had seen in this fantastic place. There was something revolting about them, and after one glance, there was an impulse to turn away; but there was another impulse to keep on looking.

They were not pleasant things to look at. No man would have wanted one of them in his house. And yet many a man would have given his soul to possess one of them. Kings would have sacrificed honor, queens would have given kingdoms, to own one of the things.

Each was about a yard in length and, including the ugly spraddling legs, almost as wide. The legs, that part of each that was not scintillating jewels, were yellow gold, finely wrought. And there was no need to count them to know that there were over a hundred.

Doc Savage, his two aids and the girl stared for almost five minutes in astonished silence.

"Scarabs," the bronze man said finally.

Edwina Day looked at him. "What?"

"Likenesses of the scarab bettle, done in jewels and gold," the bronze man explained.

"But what are they doing here?"

Doc elaborated. "The scarab beetle was worshipped by the ancient Egyptians, probably because the beetle rolled mud or dung in the shape of a ball, and the people, being worshippers of the sun which was a ball, associated the beetle with the sun and made it a holy thing. Almost entirely through the ancient Egyptian dynasties runs evidence that the scarab was a holy symbol.

They looked at the jewel-and-gold scarabs again, and so awe-inspiring was the sight that silence fell again. Tukan, to one side, spoke in low tones to a man who arrived in haste.

Then breaking the silence, Tukan said, "We must go."

"I kinda enjoy watchin' them things glitter!" Monk breathed.

Tukan grew impatient.

"A scout has brought word that Collendar and the others are marching this way," he said.

Chapter XVIII

JUDAS IN SKIRTS

The bronze man and his aids spent an hour outside the great block of stone which composed the entrance to the city in the cavern, waiting for Collendar's gang to put in an appearance.

Doc Savage, endeavoring to offer assistance in the defense, was at first ignored. But there was sound common sense behind his counsel, and he began to get attention.

He suggested that they rig a net at a considerable distance from the stone block, and one above. He offered this advice after he learned that the weapon most feared was the small time-bomb torpedoes, of which Collendar had apparently brought a large supply.

"Collendar evidently had a large number of the torpedoes constructed while he was in New York," Doc surmised.

"But why don't he stick to machine guns?" Monk asked. Instantly, he remembered the reason. "Aw, blazes! A machine gun wouldn't shoot over a rod or two in this gas."

The nets were put up. These people, it developed, fished with nets of a conventional type, and quite a number of them were on hand. They threaded them together, many hands working in haste, and fastening one edge to the bottom, sent the other edge up on floats which were filled with gases lighter than the blue gas.

Monk, whose opinion of the under-sea realm had improved to a remarkable degree, had a low opinion of the defensive measures. Monk's opinion of defensive measures of any kind was dependably low. He was a great believer in aggression.

"Why don't they get out there and fight it out?" he grumbled.

Doc had been making observations and putting inquiries. The result was an understanding of just why Tukan and his people were long on defense and short on offense.

"It has been thirty or forty centuries since these people had a war," the bronze man explained. "They live together here in perfect peace. Something like this has them baffled."

At this point, a torpedo came out of the blue gas—the things were so accurately weight-balanced that they traveled through the gas just as they would have gone through water—and tangled with the net.

It hung there, swaying slowly, like an arrow sticking in a target of loose cloth. Then it exploded, and everyone was pumping at their ears and wondering if they would ever hear again.

"I can't understand why them things sound a million times louder than they would in the air!" Edwina Day complained. "The sound hits you like a ton of bricks."

"This gas," Doc explained, "conducts sound much better than the air."

Several more torpedoes were fired, but without damaging the nets to any great extent. After this, Collendar's men came into view. They wore—and it was somewhat surprising to see these—diving suits of the all-metal type.

The only weapons they seemed to carry were hand grenades.

To Doc's astonishment, Tukan showed every indication of intending to retreat.

"The things they carry in their hands—they explode!" he explained fearfully.

It was increasingly evident that these people feared

explosives beyond all else. Collendar must have known of that.

"They cannot use the things that explode," Doc Savage pointed out, "because they must throw them. And they cannot throw them much more than the length of two arms. They will not, therefore, make use of them."

Tukan seemed much pleased. He issued orders, and a group of his men went forth to meet the invaders. Each member of the repulsing party carried a long pole, on the end of which was lashed what might have passed for a glass fruit jar full of some chemical mixture.

The exact purpose of these unique tilting lances was not evident until the two forces met. First, Collendar's men threw two grenades, which exploded. As Doc had predicted, the grenades did nothing except teach the fellows who threw them a lesson.

Then a Tukan follower rushed forward and jabbed his lance against one of the attackers. The glass jar broke. It proved to contain something similar to Thermit, a combination of chemicals which burned with terrific heat. Heat sufficient to melt through the metal diving suits in a fractional instant.

The screams of the men inside the diving suits were something not soon forgotten.

That ended the attack. Collendar's men retreated.

"That," Monk said, "was the shortest and queerest battle I ever saw fought."

There was, of course, no day or night in this weird blue realm. The inhabitants seemed to have no set hours for sleep, but exercised the rather sensible plan of sleeping when they felt like it.

The manufacturing processes necessary to life under such strange circumstances, Doc Savage learned, were conducted in an industrial "city" in another part of the crater.

The place was the interior of a volcanic crater, as the men on Doc's yacht had surmised. A crater, apparently, which was incredibly rich in chemicals. The gas which filled the place was ageless and did not depreciate with time to any extent, being replenished by a great plant in the industrial center whenever necessary.

All this Doc Savage learned as he paid visits to the diphtheria sufferers.

There had been very little surface evidence of the epidemic.

It was bad.

Someone had said that half the people were victims of the plague. That was an understatement, if anything. Deaths, in fact, had already mounted to almost a quarter of the population. Learning just how bad conditions were, Doc gained a respect for the stoicism of the people.

The bronze man inaugurated what sanitary measures he could. They were not many. He did, however, institute a quarantine and extend it to everyone except a definite group of the priests, who were to attend to fighting Collendar. Doc had enough serum to vaccinate these against diphtheria.

Doc Savage's metallic features were sober when he joined his men in the ball house where their equipment cases had been stored.

Diphtheria was no longer a terrible plague disease in the outer world. Antitoxins and vaccinations had removed its terror. But here, with antitoxin, it was as bad as it had ever been outside. Worse.

These people did not have the ordinary human being's natural immunity to disease. They were in the same boat as the Eskimos who never have common colds in their native habitat, but contract fierce colds from the first explorers who appear in their midst with one.

Doc Savage spoke to Tukan.

"Collendar wants to trade antitoxin for those jeweled scarabs in the temple?" the bronze man asked.

Tukan scowled. "That is right!"

"The scarabs are useless to you," Doc said. "You might make the trade. Later, we may be able to recover the scarabs from Collendar and Bogaccio."

Tukan glared. "Impossible!"

"They are a small price for the lives of these people who are dying!"

Tukan said, "They are the property of the Sun God!"

That was that. The gold-and-jeweled bugs belonged to their deity, and every man, woman and child, every priest and priestess, could perish before they would be surrendered. Doc gave it up.

"I wish the aid of your priests who are chemists," the bronze man said.

"Why?" asked Tukan.

The man sounded suspicious. Evidently the bronze man's suggestion to trade the gold-and-jewel scarabs for human lives had lowered Doc in his estimation.

"You can watch what we do," Doc said shortly.

They worked in the ball which held Doc's equipment cases. Their greatest difficulty was in getting the chemicals which the bronze man desired.

Tukan's men, of course, knew none of the English formulae or symbols for chemicals, and none of their ingredients had English names. It was true they could speak English, but many of the words they did not know, and chemicals were included among them.

It required hours for Doc to make his needs understood. Once Tukan comprehended, however, he dispatched a well-convoyed expedition to the manufacturing center, and this brought back the ingredients desired.

"Monk, you supervise the mixing of the chemicals," Doc directed. "Ham and myself will get them started on the mechanical devices."

The mechanical devices were simple. They were merely building flame-throwers of the type which were used in the World War.

The work took several hours.

Doc began work on the magnetic Thermit bombs next. These were more difficult, for the contact-igniting device took time. The bombs themselves consisted simply of a heavily magnetized bit of metal to which was attached a small glass container of Thermit—the chemical mixture which ignited and burned with the heat of a welding-torch flame.

The Thermit containers were lightened with a gas which would not ignite the Thermit, lightened until they were the merest shade heavier than the luminous blue gas. The problem of how to ignite the Thermit on contact was finally solved by a spring-trigger arrangement which would trip on contact, letting a small hammer smash the container.

They conducted a test. One of the Thermit bombs was released. It floated for a time, then slowly settled. Monk approached with a bit of iron on the end of a pole. The magnet on the bomb was attracted from an astonishing distance, and the trigger ignited the Thermit upon contact with the metal. They watched the intense flame melt the bit of iron.

Monk was elated.

"Brothers, this'll make it tough on them divin' suits they're wearin' for armor!" he chortled.

Doc Savage conducted further experiments to be sure the red alloy metal mesh garments worn by Tukan and his priests would not attract the magnetic bombs.

For his raid on the Collendar camp, once they found it, Doc Savage selected a dozen of Tukan's men who looked most likely to follow orders.

"I'm going along!" Edwina Day announced.

Doc assured her she wasn't. An argument developed.

"It's my brother they're holding prisoner, in case you've forgotten!" the girl said grimly.

Doc took the young woman aside, and they conferred for some time, the bronze man patiently, Edwina Day with unswerving determination.

Monk and Ham stood at a distance, watched, and laid wagers about who would win the argument. Ham bet on Doc. He lost.

"She is going along," Doc said, returning with the girl.

He did not sound very crestfallen.

The guards at the line of hanging torpedo nets went through a ritual as they took their departure from that point. The performance consisted of a good deal of wailing and making of cabalistic symbols, following which each man dictated a message to an individual who was apparently the equivalent of a public stenographer.

Monk squinted at the notes which the stenographer was making, but they were in hieroglyphics and meant nothing to him.

He made inquiries.

"They are indicating what distribution they wish to make of their personal belongings in case they are so unfortunate as not to return," Tukan explained.

"You mean they're makin' out their wills?" Monk demanded.

"Exactly."

Monk took a couple of large gulps of luminous blue gas.

"All I can say," he muttered, "is that this is the first army I ever saw make a public formality of makin' out their wills before they went to war."

All personal fortunes having been satisfactorily routed to descendants, the raiding part got under way again. They crawled under the torpedo net, formed a tight group, and marched.

When they had gone about a hundred yards, Doc Savage called a halt and set up a supersentitive listening device. This consisted of a highly directional parabolic microphone which could be rotated, an amplifier and a headset. He turned the device slowly and listened.

Noises which he heard to the right and ahead were fairly sure to indicate Collendar's group. All the other inhabitants of this weird world had been concentrated, either in the city of the ball-shaped buildings, or in the industrial town.

Doc Savage removed the headset, pointed toward where Collendar's crew was located, and put questions to his red-clothed allies.

"Is there any kind of building over there in which Collendar might be camped?" the bronze man asked.

There was a storehouse at the spot. From the description of the building, Doc judged it was an acceptable blockhouse.

"Gonna be hard to get 'em out of there," was Monk's opinion.

Doc asked about openings in the place. There was, he learned, a number of embrasures, put there for ventilating purposes. They were not, however, large enough to admit a man. The holes would permit passage of the magnetic Thermit bombs, however.

Doc Savage scooped up a handful of fine sand, held it over his head and released it. The stuff drifted slightly in, slowly floating downward.

The luminous gas, then, moved in currents. There was nothing mysterious about that. The ocean overhead moved in a current, and friction of the sea water against the gas was certain to give the gas movement, also. The stuff would move with the sea overhead, and move the opposite direction on the bottom where they stood.

The twelve red-garmented assistants carried heavy cylinders containing the stupefying chemical with which Doc and his men had been overcome in the diving tank.

This stuff, Doc had learned, was used, in addition to the nets, in fishing. It was released in the sea to overcome fish, just as the natives of Central and South America put similar stuff in their native streams.

"Here is the plan," Doc Savage announced. "We will release the stupefying chemical. Doctor Collendar, Snig Bogaccio and the others will naturally put on their metal diving suits as a defensive measure. Then we will turn loose a few of the magnetic Thermit bombs, get them into the place, and the metal diving suits will attract them."

Ham looked a trifle queer. He was remembering Doc Savage's policy, unalterably enforced since the beginning of their association, of never taking human lives.

Doc said, "The Thermit burns are not likely to prove fatal."

When everyone else was engaged in the preparations, the man in the red cloak approached Edwina Day.

The man was one of the dozen priests whom Tukan had brought along. In appearance, he differed little from the others, being tall, with a cream-colored skin, and a lengthy thin-boned look. If anything, his eyes were more dark and intent, his manner more earnest.

At the call for volunteers for this expedition, he had been the first to step forth.

He drew near Edwina Day, then turned slowly to make sure no one else was in earshot.

"You are killing my brother!" he said in a low voice.

Edwina Day had been thinking about her brother, wondering what Collendar would do to him when straits became desperate. The girl gave a violent start and became shades paler. Her first thought was that she had not heard correctly.

"What did you say?" she asked queerly.

The red priest's eyes smouldered darkly. "I was designated to bring you a message," he muttered.

Edwina Day stared at him. "I don't understand."

"Your brother will die," the man said.

The girl's breath caught in her throat. Her body, from shoulders to waist, seemed to shrink.

"I—but—" She could not get the words out.

"You can save his life, however," the red priest continued. "If Harry Day dies, his blood will be on your hands, because you can save him."

Edwina Day's hands became claws that dug at her frock. "What—what do you mean?"

"You can go to Collendar," the man said, "and guide him to this spot. With a surprise attack, he can take this Doc Savage. It is his only chance."

The girl was tight and trembling for a long time. Her nerves were like charged wires. Her teeth tormented her lips until they grew white from punishment.

"I—I couldn't—get away," she said finally.

"You can tell them you have beome frightened and are going back to the city."

Edwina Day's mouth made shapes for a while.

"Why—don't—you warn Collendar?" she asked.

The red priest shrugged. "My fellows suspect me, and they are watching. They suspect the truth: that I am one of Collendar's group. They would not let me slip away. See? They are watching."

It was true. Edwina Day saw this with a glance that she tried hard to make casual.

The priest spoke slowly, distinctly.

"Your brother," he said, "will die. That was Collendar's word."

A chill shaking seemed to begin at the girl's lips and spread through her whole body.

When she got the shaking controlled, she went to Doc Savage.

"I am frightened," she choked. "I am going back to the city. I can make it alone."

She looked scared enough.

Chapter XIX

DEATH IN THE BLUE

Doctor Hugo Collendar, looking pleasant and handsome said, "By all means, let the young lady in."

Edwina Day came in. The swimming gestures which she used to help herself through the heavy gas were stiff, unnatural. The blue tint of the vapor made her coloring more stark.

She looked around quickly, but she was only in a long room which smelled of stored seaweed.

Doctor Collendar smiled at her. He had a trick of smiling when he was in a cruel mood.

He asked, "Just why did you come?"

The girl jerked words out by twos and threes.

"One of the priests—told me—my brother—you'd kill him—if I didn't help—trap Doc Savage!"

Collendar took a deep breath. Took it as if he were sampling perfume that sold for forty dollars an ounce.

"So that worked," he murmured. "I was afraid it wouldn't." He looked at the girl and lifted his thin upper lip off his white teeth. "I had a better opinion of your courage!"

129

The girl did not wince. She only looked cowed, desperate.

"My brother!" she gasped.

Collendar shook his head. "My bargain stands. Show me how to get rid of Doc Savage, and you'll get your brother. Furthermore, I'll see that you both get out of this place. I'll put you ashore in some port."

Edwina Day began to tremble. Suddenly, she sprang forward and began to beat her fists against Doctor Collendar.

"My brother!" she shrieked. "You've killed him!"

Collendar caught her wrists. "He's alive, you little idiot!"

The girl began screaming. Her shrieks, changed in quality by the dense gas, were somehow more awful than they would have been in the open air.

"You've killed him!" she screeched.

Doctor Collendar struggled with her. The girl screeched, moaned, screeched again.

"Damn it!" Collendar snarled. "Snig, show her the blasted brother!"

Snig Bogaccio was a swart, stout man with too pretty a face for his ugly body. The plastic surgery operation had done that for him. He led Edwina Day into another room.

Harry Day lay on the floor, bound securely. He looked as if he had been beaten a good deal. He peered at his sister.

"Edwina!" he muttered. "You—you sold out!"

Then he fainted.

Major John Renwick was on the floor near by. Renny's huge fists were roped together, as were his ankles. Long Tom Roberts was also on the floor, bound. They looked at the girl.

"Doc!" Renny rumbled.

"He's—all—right," the girl said haltingly.

Renny took a deep breath. "You sold him out, eh?"

The girl's nod was hardly perceptible. But it was agony.

Renny licked his lips. "Holy cow! It's tough, kid. But nobody blames you." The big-fisted engineer scowled. "I'd probably sell out for Doc, too. A brother's the same thing."

For the attack on Doc Savage, Collendar and Bogaccio took all their men. Edwina Day was the cause of that. Or what she told them caused it. She explained that Doc Savage was going to gas the place and get them into their diving suit armors, then send in magnetic Thermit bombs which the steel suits would attract, and burn them to a crisp. She laid it on heavy.

Snig Bogaccio had thirteen of his own men along. He did not seem happy about the unlucky number. Seven of the Judas priests completed the group, exclusive of the leaders, Bogaccio and Collendar. They outnumbered Doc's party, and they were desperate.

One of Bogaccio's thugs had been badly damaged by one of the grenades which he had tried to throw in the earlier battle. He was not fit for war. So they left him to guard the prisoners, Harry Day, Renny and Long Tom.

The men then walked out of the warehouse fortress like men leaving something they had just learned was a tomb.

Edwina Day led the way.

When they had circled, and were coming up through the semi-opaque blue fog to a spot behind where she had left Doc Savage making his attack preparations, the girl stopped them.

"He's there," she said. She pointed.

Collendar nodded.

"We'll get him," he said.

Bogaccio nodded, too.

"Youse said it!" he said.

The words did not go well with his handmade face.

"Spread out!" Collendar ordered. "We'll get them before they can turn those magnetic Thermit bombs loose."

They spread out. They went forward. Before long, they saw a reddish protuberance on the ground. That was all it was in the blue gas, just a protuberance. They went a little closer, and it began to resemble figures closely grouped.

Collendar beckoned the others close.

"They're gathered for a powwow!" he said. "Probably final orders before the attack. We'll take 'em by surprise!"

He sounded excited and ugly.

The group went forward. They went forward until they could almost touch the clustered red figures. Collendar did touch one of them. He pushed it over.

It was a red alloy mesh garment full of sand. Just a dummy.

Collendar said twenty or thirty wild words. None of them were understandable.

Edwina Day had lagged a score of yards behind. She was farther away than that now. She was run-swimming in a mad thirst for distance from that spot.

The loud-speaker on the ground among the dummies began to talk. It was the speaker off Doc's radio equipment. A wire ran from it and off over the ground and through the cultivated food-type seaweed. No one had noticed the wire.

The loud-speaker said, *"Put down your weapons! Take off those diving suits!"*

It was Doc Savage's voice.

Collendar screamed. Screamed noise at first. Then words.

"Go get them!" he bawled. "Follow that wire!"

The loud-speaker crashed, *"Keep away from the wire! It is—"*

Collendar never heard what it was. He was too mad to hear anything. He roared and rushed along the wire, and his men followed him. That was unfortunate. They did not hear Doc add that the magnetic Thermit bombs had been strewn along the wire—just in case.

Only about a third of the gang died from the Thermit bomb burns. Collendar and Bogaccio had the luck of the devil with them, and didn't die.

But they were all easily captured.

Chapter XX

MINDS AT PEACE

Tukan, the high priest, was a stubborn man. He was a good man at his job, and although he believed implicitly in the tomfoolery and rituals which he went through daily in the name of the creed of his ancestors, it was a harmless kind of thing. Probably it did a deal of good. At least, it kept the minds of his subjects occupied, hence probably helped keep down the percentage of devilment.

But he was stubborn.

As Monk said, "What we need is a mule driver!"

Monk said that after listening to Doc Savage argue for four solid hours, they should be permitted to leave the strange underwater realm. And Tukan said, "No!" as firmly at the end as he had at the beginning.

Doc's arguments seemed weighty enough. As the bronze man pointed out, they had eliminated the menace of Doctor Collendar, Snig Bogaccio and their men.

The Collendar menace elimination had been made most complete, incidentally, when the bronze man finished a delicate brain operation on Collendar, Bogaccio and each of the men, and wiped out all memory of the past.

Tukan had been an interested observer of the operation. He was suitably astonished when Collendar and the others, upon recovering, were told they had always been here in the underwater world, and believed it.

True, Doc Savage admitted, pretty Edwina Day had helped him overcome Collendar's crowd. Collendar hadn't known that the girl was to lead him into a trap. Doc had made that arrangement with the young woman long before Collendar's crooked ally approached her.

The bronze man, who had painstakingly formed a habit of overlooking no bets, had foreseen that an effort to make the girl sell out for her brother's life was something that could happen.

Tukan gave one of his rare smiles after that.

"Miss Day," he said, "is a charming person."

Monk and Ham still thought so, too. Although Tukan's priestesses were not bad, Monk and Ham concentrated their efforts on Edwina Day. It was some time before they began to suspect the reason for their lack of success. They came upon the young lady helping Tukan improve his English.

They had found the antitoxin, of course, and Doc Savage, working furiously, had stemmed the diphtheria epidemic, and eventually stopped it completely. Then he gave Tukan's more intelligent priests some instructions about fighting the more common diseases. This took about six weeks.

The six weeks were lazy. When they had gone by, Monk and the others suddenly awakened to a realization.

They were eating a meal.

"This ain't so bad," Monk remarked.

The others stopped eating and stared at each other. It really wasn't bad. That was the astonishing thing. They had fallen into the ways of the strange place, and forgetting some of the conveniences of the outer world, and becoming accustomed to some of the greater conveniences here, they had, almost literally, gone native.

They were worried when they went to Doc.

"Yes," the bronze man said. "I have stopped feeling sorry for these people. It would not be bad to live here forever. But at the same time, we should leave." He got to his feet. "The lifeboats from the yacht reached the

European coast, and the men chartered a steamer and are standing by overhead."

"What about the steamer *Sea Mist*, that Collendar hired?" Ham asked.

"Turned up in port and reported Collendar and his men went down in diving suits and never came up," Doc replied. "The men on the steamer did not know what it was all about."

"I'll bet the newspapers thought that was a crazy one," Monk chuckled.

Doc said, "We will talk to Tukan again."

Tukan said, "I will be sorry to lose you."

The shock made Monk sit down where there wasn't any place to sit down. "You're gonna let us go?"

Tukan smiled. "Yes."

"But," Monk croaked, "why the change of heart?"

Tukan's smile got back against his ears.

"Where there is love in one's heart," he said, "there is also warmth and kindness toward fellow men."

Monk peered closely at Tukan. He thought the fellow sounded like a forty-year-old calf. There wasn't any such thing as a forty-year-old calf, of course, but the idea occurred to Monk.

"I am in love," Tukan said, "with Miss Day."

For the first time since he had been here, the blue gas choked Monk.

"You—" he said. "Uh—"

Tukan turned to Doc Savage. "Miss Day has told me much about you and your strange work, and because I trust her, rather than I would trust any man, I am letting you go free and depending upon you to never reveal the whereabouts of this place."

"No one will ever know," Doc Savage promised.

Monk found his voice.

"I won't have it!" he howled.

"Won't have what?" Tukan asked curiously.

"That girl is sellin' herself to buy our freedom!" Monk roared. "She's marryin' you so you'll turn us loose! She's marryin'—"

Monk choked again. He regretted that, because he had a lot more to say, much of it about the fact that he knew Tukan was sixty years old.

Tukan sighed deeply.

"Miss Day," he said, "is not marrying me. She is going with you and her brother."

"Not marrying you?" Monk swallowed. "Uh—why not?"

Tukan's sigh was the deepest one he had heaved.

"Why not? Because I have six wives already." He frowned. "Although that seems no reason at all to me."

DOC SAVAGE

To the world at large, Doc Savage is a strange, mysterious figure of glistening bronze skin and golden eyes. To his fans he is the greatest adventure hero of all time, whose fantastic exploits are unequaled for hair-raising thrills, breathtaking escapes, blood-curdling excitement!

☐	THE EVIL GNOME	2134	$1.25
☐	THE MAN OF BRONZE	6352	$1.25
☐	THE STONE MAN	6419	$1.25
☐	THE THOUSAND HEADED MAN	6471	$1.25
☐	THE RED TERRORS	6486	$1.25
☐	DOC SAVAGE: HIS APOCALYPTIC LIFE	8834	$1.25
☐	THE PHANTOM CITY	10119	$1.25
☐	THE MYSTIC MULLAH	10120	$1.25
☐	FEAR CAY	10121	$1.25
☐	LAND OF ALWAYS NIGHT	10122	$1.25
☐	FANTASTIC ISLAND	10125	$1.25
☐	QUEST OF QUI	10126	$1.25

Bantam Book Catalog

It lists over a thousand money-saving bestsellers originally priced from $3.75 to $15.00 —bestsellers that are yours now for as little as 60¢ to $2.95!

The catalog gives you a great opportunity to build your own private library at huge savings!

So don't delay any longer—send us your name and address and 25¢ (to help defray postage and handling costs).
